TALES GOING NOWHERE

Jaelyn Phillips

b POZ!
PUBLISHING

ISBN-13: 979-8-9853031-0-0

Cover design by: bPOZI Publishing
Printed in the United States of America

For Big Tate, Mash-taters, and Mama't. I couldn't have done it without y'all

CONTENTS

PROLOGUE

Glenndale isn't your average town. Sure, they have a mayor, people to govern, and a bank like every other town. It's smack dab in the middle of Nowhere County with a population that changes like the weather. There have been strange phenomena happening in Glenndale ever since it was established, but this past year for them has proven to be stranger. Stuck in a time loop, what's a town to do? No way out, but to venture further into Glenndale, and hope to get out soon.

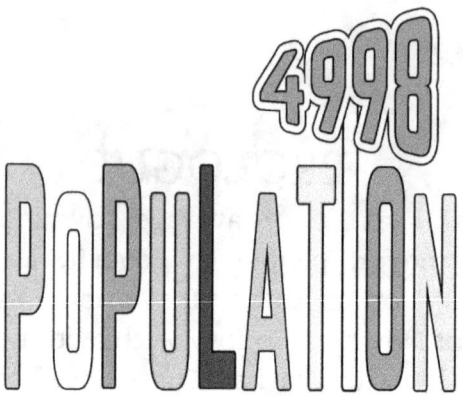

POPULATION 4998

The population used to be 5,000 even, but after the car accident, it's been reduced to 4,998.

1. population: 4,998

There's a town called Glenndale. It was renamed after the mayor who unfortunately died in a car accident. The population used to be 5,000 even, but after the car accident, it's been reduced to 4,998.

Glenndale is a town consisting of some seemingly ordinary people, but don't be fooled by their simplicity. Each and every single one of them is holding a secret. Some that are true, some they want to believe are true, and the ones that no one can ever know about.

Not only do they have secrets, but they also gossip. It's roughly a small town and you can try and hide your secret, or privacy, but word will get out by the end of the day. They get along for the most part, despite being on top of each other, but if they can help it they'll get out of this town as soon as the opportunity is given.

Glenndale is in the middle of Nowhere County. A petition by the teenagers of the surrounding towns back in the day wanted to name the county Nowhere as a running joke. At the time it was funny, and if a tourist were to come to Glenndale, for whatever reason, they'd get a little laugh out of it. The joke ran stale after several years to say you live in the middle of nowhere.

However, there are a few people who love Glenndale. To them there's nothing outside of the woods for them, and they're content where they are.

That or they might be scared to what might happen to them if they try and leave this town. Who knows?

Though the woods can be beautiful, there's something about them that's unsettling.

2. the woods

The woods surround Glenndale. It wraps itself around the town, leaving only patches of open spaces and fields for the farmers. The trees are thick, reaching as far as a two-story building, but under certain lights, the woods look harmless. They hold grazing deer with the gentleness to approach and even pet. The sunlight peeking through the leaves makes it feel enchanted.

Though the woods can be beautiful, there's something about them that's unsettling. It holds both secrets and darkness that no one has dared to understand. The deep woods of Glenndale can be haunting to some. It's the one part of town that remains untouched, and to those who enter go with a sense of respect or face the consequences.

Rarely do people stay the night in the woods; troop leaders don't even take their scouts for camping to the woods. Lately, the woods haven't been safe at night.

It's usually the tourists who face the music with the woods. A lot more tourists have been coming ever since those kids returned from their trip passing through the thickets of trees. Most tourists take the warning well and leave the woods before the sun goes down. However, there is always an exception.

* * *

One incident involved a few college students from out of town. They ignored the sign about the stone arch near the entrance of the woods that those twenty kids and their teacher went missing. They had passed under the arch for a camping trip ten years ago, and haven't returned since. Some of these students were too scared to go under it after reading the sign while others pushed one another as a joke. They ran under the ruins and ran back out laughing.

It was late when they set up their campsite and some were already drunk. One of the guys wandered away from their fire to relieve himself. He kicked a couple of beer cans along the way, while his friends talked on and on about what if the spirits were true. Would they come for revenge, they laughed.

Ten minutes passed and their friend wasn't back. They thought he might be lost, so they went looking around for him, calling out his name, and after while. They heard a scream and ran towards the sound.

One of the girls discovered him with eight arrows prodding out of his body like quills.

The college students yelled at the officers later on. They told them what happened; some yelled that they'd sue Glenndale for all its money. They left with their friend's body and the ambulance to escort them away from town.

* * *

They never did return. Perhaps they realized that they didn't have a case to make, that they were all drunk, or how the locals warned them. But maybe they were too afraid to go through the woods again.

Later on, the medical staff of the hospital outside of town spoke with Dr. Oak, the top director of the hospital in Glenndale.

The arrows, based on the sampling of the material used to make them, were made over 100 years ago. That the arrowheads were worn down over and over after each use.

The staff member also mentioned to Dr. Oak how there was another sample of blood found on the arrowhead. A sample that didn't match the young man. The origins of this blood could be dated back to be 100 years old.

Pick any booth you want,
but never pick the booth in
the back right corner.

3. the booth

There's a diner that everyone goes to. Whether it be a quick cup of coffee, birthday parties, or even last-minute cakes, the diner was the place for it all. Though popular, be warned about where you sit.

The stools near the counter are always good. They're perfect for having room for yourself, but if you have kids it's a game of risk. No one sits at those center tables unless they have to, so that leaves the booths. Pick any booth you want, but never pick the booth in the back right corner.

❋ ❋ ❋

"I heard that someone died in that booth," one of the twins says.

A group of high schoolers are sitting in the diner late one night. Their discussion somehow ends up at the back right booth; the one with the lights off above it.

"Ugh, yawn. Been there, heard that all before," the girl with the bleached cropped blonde hair says, "What? They died choking on a carrot?"

"Oh Vivian your lack of imagination is

disturbing," he says back.

She flips him off.

"I'm thinking that a man got a call that his wife passed. He was eating a burger and had previous heart problems, so he heard the news and died of a heart attack," he finishes.

"Very realistic, but it was probably something supernatural," one of the girls suggests, "I'm thinking something like bad karma."

"Oh geez. You all should be my writing consultants with all this creative energy." Vivian says waving her hands.

"You wouldn't be able to afford us. We charge by the minute." The girl with the glasses mocks.

They're about the only ones there besides the waitress and two men at the counter. Suddenly, the door opens and in walks a young man about the group's age.

"Hey, isn't that Alex?" The other twin asks, looking over his brother's head.

"Shh, shut up or he'll hear you," the girl with the glasses sinks, checking quickly to see if he heard them.

They all coo at her as Alex approaches the register.

"Oh leave the poor girl alone," Vivian says waving them off, "but what's to stop us from saying hi?"

They call out to him and wave him over.

"You'll pay for this," the girl says, sinking

even further as he looks over.

"You'll thank us later," the other girl says.

He walks over.

"Hey guys, how's it going?" Alex asks, looking around the table. He notices the girl with the glasses.

"Oh, hey." He smiles.

"Hi Alex," she sits up, still not meeting his eyes.

"How's the book?"

"Hmm?" She briefly meets his gaze.

"Oh, you know. We were supposed to have a book club over it." He laughs, rubbing the back of his head.

"Oh right yea, it's good so far," she mumbles to her hands, pulling her sleeves to cover them.

"So what brings you guys out so late?" He asks, bringing a chair over to their booth.

"Hanging out, but then we were theorizing what could've happened at that booth." One of the twins points back at the booth.

"Yea, and Vivian over here keeps going into writing mode, telling us our theories are wrong."

"I can't help it if your stories are just plain boring," she says as they ball up their napkins, throwing them at her.

"What do you think Alex?" The girl with the glasses asks.

"Hmm, something simple. An older angry man comes to the diner to die and haunt this place," he shrugs, looking at her for confirmation.

"Dude that's morbid but so cool." One of the twins reaches across to high-five him.

"Alex, you know I love you dearly, but that was so boring," Vivian says dramatically.

"I'll tell y'all the story." One of the men from the counter says, turning to face them.

"I've been going to this diner ever since I was a kid. I've seen lots of things, but this one'll stick with you." He mumbles, gazing at them with coal eyes.

The group goes quiet as they listen closely.

"I was out with my friends like y'all. We were in that booth."

He points to the booth right next to the back corner one.

"We were having fun, not a care in the world when two guys came in wearing trench coats and sat down. I remembered that one of them ordered a black coffee. The smell still ripe in my nose every time I drink a cup.

My back was turned away from them so I couldn't see, but I remembered they talked low. Maybe ten minutes later, one of them gets up. I heard him put down some change and walk out. The waitress didn't clear the table 'cause the other guy was still there."

He pauses to take a sip of his own coffee. The group waiting for him to set it back down and continue. He gulps, wipes his mouth and carries on.

"A few seconds later, the smell hit me. It was

strong, and that's when I looked over to see him. He was slumped over. You might've thought he was asleep. The waitress did and she tapped him to wake him up. He fell forward, blood pooling on the floor and table. I can still smell it, it mixed in with the smell of black coffee."

He finishes, turning back around. The group looks at him. They then look at the booth, and then at each other.

"Order for Alex." The waitress yells, ringing a bell that makes them jump.

"Well, uh that's me," he says slowly getting up.

He waves goodbye, they watch him leave, and sit in silence not really in the mood for dessert anymore.

"Well, let's get out of here, yes?" One of the twins wipes his hands on a napkin before looking at all of them. They all nod in agreement, walking out quieter than they came in, avoiding the man's eyes as they left.

The man turns back to stare into his cup, taking another gulp and wiping at his nose as the waitress comes back to fill it up again.

He forgot to mention to the kids, probably for the best, on how when they tried to clean up the body. No matter how hard they tried the blood wouldn't come up. That's why the light was low over in the corner.

"This town keeps getting
weirder and weirder."

4. the blue moon film festival

Glenndale can be a simple, quiet town, but it's mostly known for being odd. All of the other towns in Nowhere County have their usual 4th of July parades, they have their typical Christmas pageants, and summer carnivals. Well Glenndale does all of this, but they tend to add things that don't really exist.

Sometimes they make up holidays or throw in random festivals if you ask the mayor nice enough. There's been apple picking competitions, there have been random music festivals with only a day's notice, and there have been times like rainbow week.

This year marked the second birthday of the Blue Moon Film Festival. It's an event that would happen about every two and a half years on the night of a blue moon; hence the name.

It was the idea of a film student who wanted to encourage other people who share his passion to make movies.

People went all out this year, some going as far as covering their entire bodies in blue paint.

There's a tall gentleman in a blue checkered suit, top hat, and shiny monocle handing out blue moon balloons to all the kids.

Some kids dress in something blue too, but a majority stay in their regular costumes, because this year the Blue Moon Film Festival falls on the exact date of Halloween.

* * *

"This town keeps getting weirder and weirder." A man comments dressed up as Popeye the sailor man.

"I think this town is wonderful," the woman next to him says, she dresses as Olive Oyl, "This town is magical."

"Alright Olive Oyl, let's enjoy ourselves a blue moon," he says in Popeye's voice.

The woman laughs at his attempt and holds his hand as they walk into the festival.

This year is a little strange to hold the Blue Moon Festival because it means people have to decide. They either go to their Halloween parties or the festival; that or leave an event early for the other.

Teenagers have their Halloween parties, parents take their kids to collect candy, and those without kids have to hand them out. Some neighborhoods decided that they'd turn out their lights at around eight to get to the festival. That worked for most parents so that way they could take their kids home and they enjoy the festival. This, however, is a problem for the babysitters who had to watch them; missing both events.

"This blows," Vivian says, putting away her phone.

She's dresses as a blue bearded pirate with stars sprinkled in her beard.

"What does?" One of the twins asks, dressed as one of the Grady sisters from *The Shining*.

"Morgan said she can't make it 'cause she's stuck babysitting," she says, crossing her arms.

"Well, almost every parent is out tonight. It'd be unsafe, especially now to leave your kids alone." One of the girls who dresses as Violet from *Charlie and the Chocolate Factory* after she turned into a blueberry, says at her side.

"I know, it's so unfair though, she's getting paid like 45 an hour or something. I totally should've been a babysitter," she mumbles.

"I'm sorry, did you say 45 an hour?" The other twin dressed as the other Grady sister says, nearly choking on his blue lemonade, "Hell, I'll babysit for her."

He makes a move to walk away, but his brother grabs his arm.

"Oh come on Viv. We can still have fun, and we'll bring Morgan some blue cheese fries and a balloon for her kids. Then you can show her your costume, cause we know you worked so hard on it." The girl with the glasses says, rubbing her friend's shoulder.

She dresses as a sleek superhero covered in yellow, red, and blue. A blue mask with white eyes to match. She even let Morgan chalk her hair a deep blue and slick it back before leaving.

Vivian laughs a little.

"You'd do that for me?"

"Of course, you would just owe me a lemonade."

"Where is all this confidence coming from? Certainly not the moon?" She asks as they all link arms, walking deeper into the festival.

"I'm the protector of the moon, of course, it's where I get my confidence and powers." The girl bumps back.

They all find a nice spot on the grass after getting their food and drinks, waiting for the first film to show. The moon high in the sky, shining over all of them like a huge spotlight, setting the stage for what's to come.

THE FIELD TRIP

They pass through the woods, thankfully during the day.

5. the field trip

Now it's a fact that every seventh-grader in Glenndale goes on a two-day camping trip. The school allows this and parents are fine with this because the camping spot is inexpensive and it's been the same spot for the past 50 years.

The issue is that it's hard to keep track of over two hundred middle schoolers, so they divide the classes to see who goes on what weekend.

This weekend trip would be for Mr. Carson's homeroom class of 18, plus the two from a different class that couldn't make it a few weeks ago.

"Alright class, two others will be joining us due to personal circumstances. I want you all to be respectful to me, them, yourselves, and the great outdoors with which we are about to become one."

"I'd rather become one with my PlayStation," one of the kids cracks at his friends in the back. They all snickered silently.

"Listen. Hey, listen. I need you all to make sure that you have all you need for tomorrow. That means check the list I made. Bring all medication and get it checked with me, and besides your phones, all devices should be gone. Okay?" He says.

"Okay," they all mumble.

"Okay?!" He says louder.

"Okay," they say back even louder.

The bell rings and they all file out.

"I don't know why we can't go to Disney World. We totally raised enough for some of us to go anyways," the kid with the curly red hair whines.

"We raised that money for charity and to feed kids across America," one of the girls responds to him.

"No, I understand Del's point. Why does every one of us have to go on this stupid camping trip?" The funny kid throws his hands up, "What is it? A rite of passage?"

"It'll be fun, come on guys," the blonde kid says.

"Of course you say that wonder boy, you're a true American. Chop wood, hunt deer, and drink beer. AMERICA," he says back with a salute.

They laugh and the blonde kid takes a fake swing at him.

"All I'm saying is that this might be fun."

They all wave him off, but the girl with the long, curly hair sticks back with the blonde boy.

"I hope it'll be fun, I'm gonna miss Gina's birthday party for this," she says, hugging her sides.

"We can get her later. Besides, maybe I could teach you how to start a fire," he says, bumping her shoulder playfully. She smiles up at him.

"That'd be nice," she blushes back.

"Hey lovebirds come on, I'd like to go home," someone says.

They both look away and walk to catch up to the group.

The next day, they all fly past their classes, too excited to focus and teachers too tired to calm them down. By the end of the day, parents line up with hugs, snacks, and last-minute supplies. Some of the kids act all tough and avoid their parent's kisses, saying they'll be back by Sunday. A few friends stay after to wish their friends off, having already gone on their trips.

"Thank God y'all aren't showing up to the game tomorrow. Coach finally decided to cancel," one of the kid's soccer mates says to them.

"Cause we carry the team," the funny kid puffs his chest and a few of the girls hit him.

They all wave goodbye and pile on the bus.

"Where's the bus driver?" The girl next to David asks.

"Good afternoon class, ready to hit the road?" Mr. Carson gets on the bus and sits in the driver's seat.

"Oh God, we're all doomed," Del shouts.

They all start to complain.

"Listen, class, I was a bus driver in a different life. I'll get us there in time, and," he points up looking through the rearview mirror, "I'll let you all request songs, as long as they aren't inappropriate. Pick carefully, 'cause I was also a singer in a different life."

As they pull out, some kids stick their heads out the window to wave goodbye until they can't see anyone anymore. They pass through the woods, thankfully during the day.

"Should be there in about two hours," he says.

That was the last thing he said before passing under the big stone arch.

Not once did a cop step foot through those doors; that is until today.

6. the hat shop

The Hat Shop is a front. Everyone in town knows it, and it's not like people don't buy hats. It's just too odd and too obvious to be anything but a front for something else.

It's been in business for years and maybe a handful of people have gone in per year. The Hat Shop has hats, go figure. They have church hats, baseball hats, cowboy hats, even drinking hats. They got it all, but it's an obvious face behind something else.

The town has always speculated on it. Are the owners in on it, or are the people that go into the store "buyers" of something illegal? They can never find out because as obvious as it is, it's hard to prove anything without evidence. Glenndale left it alone, call it lack of motivation or not wanting to get involved, but the Hat Shop lived on. Not once did a cop step foot through those doors; that is until today.

* * *

The bell rings over the door as someone steps in. The man behind the counter reading the newspaper spots another man walking in over the top of his paper.

"Can I help you with something....," he trails off as he sets down his paper to look at the man in his very real police uniform and gun, "Officer." He finishes, sitting up straighter.

"Oh, you don't have to address me that way. I'm just looking around," The Cop says.

He starts to whistle while he walks around, picking up and setting hats back down as he moves.

"Alright, I'll be here if you need help." The owner lets his hand hover on the button under the counter and sends a text to his friend.

He keeps a casual eye on the Cop and folds his paper in half, looking down but keeping the officer in his peripheral vision. The cop makes one round through the store, and every time he looks over at the man behind the counter, so did the man. And they would both look away immediately. The Cop sighs and heads over. The man rests his hand on the counter, the other with the paper near the button.

"What can I do for you, officer?" He asks as calmly as he can muster.

The Cop holds up his hands.

"Listen, there's an elephant in the room and I have to say it. I know," he says.

"Know what?" The man asks. He's sweating now.

"I know that you know that I am an

officer of the law... and I am without a hat," he says looking ashamed. Head bowed, wringing his sweaty hands.

The man furrows his brow and sets the paper down, flattening both his hands on the counter now.

"I'm sorry, I don't...," he trails off.

"You don't have to act surprised. I know what it looks like, " he says, shaking his head, "A cop who can't even keep a hold of his cap shouldn't be protecting citizens like you."

"Officer, you shouldn't be beating yourself up too much. It happens to all of us," the man says relaxing as this cop wasn't here for him, "Just this morning, I lost the keys to this place." The man continues.

The Cop chuckles a little.

"So how'd you open up shop?"

"Always have a spare." The man says revealing an extra key attached to a chain around his neck.

"If only hats worked like that," he sighs.

"Well, is there anything I can do?"

"Exactly why I came. I was wondering if I could buy a police cap, just until I find my old one?"

"You got it, wait here. We should have one in the back," he says walking to the back room behind the counter.

He heads out and down a few flights of stairs. He knocks, then opens the door to a room. The unmistakable smell of roosters hangs in the air, his friend sits at a table while the man walks into another small closet where actual hats were.

"Did he leave, is he on to us?" His friend calls after him.

"Nah, he's an idiot cop who lost his hat." He laughs.

"Should we call it off tonight?" He replies, shuffling money.

"Nah, I'll make sure he doesn't come around again," he says, leaving with a box of hats.

He closes the door and goes back the way he came. Back behind the counter, he hands the cop a few caps to try. The officer reaches for his wallet to pay, but the owner holds up his hands.

"It's on the house. Thanks for serving and protecting our streets," he says, handing him the cap, "plus it's a spare hat now," he says with a smile, laying it on thick.

The officer tips his new hat. A buzz on his shoulder walkie-talkie alerts him.

"Gotta run, have a great day sir."

The Cop walks off and the owner goes back to his paper; feeling mighty proud of himself.

THE STONE ARCH

...tear it down or leave it up.

7. the stone arch

There's a stone arch in the woods, and not a single townsperson knows how it got there or who made it. It's a great big arch, gray, cracked with age, yet big enough to have a semi pass under it. Much like most of the woods, it remains untouched. The only issue is that now the town must decide to tear it down or leave it up.

* * *

"A repeat of what happened, can't happen again." A councilwoman says.

"Agreed." Another member chimes in.

They all look to where the Mayor would've been, but she's not in today. Lately, with this new council, she has felt like taking charge and stepping up in politics. If she were here now, she would convince them all that one would be better than the other with little to no argument.

"I disagree." Someone speaks, breaking their collective gaze on the Mayor's chair.

With that comment, the first debate begins.

"Why do you think that we shouldn't tear down something that has brought trauma and misfortune to this town?"

"One word: Sacred," he says leaning forward, "we don't know what's in those woods or where that arch came from. It's probably been there before this was even a town."

"Councilman Danvers, please reassure me that you don't believe in ghost stories." The woman says, rubbing her temple.

"I don't, but we can't overlook the events that have taken place in my time here. There's something that we don't understand about that arch, and I'd rather not be the one to find out."

A few more words and statements are called out before one woman stands up.

"I have to agree with Councilman Danvers and Harrison. This is a force we haven't dealt with," she shuffles through some of her papers, "I went to the hospital to interview Dr. Oak. He told me of the incident in the woods with the arrows. It sounds impossible, but this town has proven to deal with the impossible," she says.

"But, what we do know is that whatever that arch is, it's an attraction. Tourist rates have gone up due to it. What if someone passes through and something happens. We could have a lawsuit against us," someone on the opposing team says.

"But much like the signs about the woods at night, we can warn others about the seriousness of the arch."

"That's not gonna stop people. Look at those kids with the arrows. Didn't stop them."

A few more arguments are thrown back and forth before someone raps a gavel.

"We'll table this issue until further notice, it's almost noon. Let's take a break and we'll pick up with another topic."

They all break and head out in every direction.

"We don't know much about this town anymore, huh?" A couple of council members walk out side by side.

"It doesn't seem like it," she sighs, "it's just so weird being back here."

"I get what you mean: arrows, scarecrows, moon festivals, and a stone arch that we as kids kicked a bunch causing such a mess." He shrugs.

"I guess when you're younger you hardly think of this town as weird."

"Yeah." He nods.

They walk until they reach a restaurant. They order their food and take a seat at the window.

"I just don't get that arch. I don't," she says pushing her straw around, "we threw rocks at it and watched birds fly under it. Nothing happened"

The man looks up, an idea in his head.

"That's it. We need proof of something supernatural happening. So much so that it would scare some sense into the others."

"I'm not sure." She looks at him, but fiddles with her straw.

"We have nothing to lose. They might just

tear it down anyways, but we have to try."

She looks in the direction of the woods.

"Alright, but we have 30 minutes."

They grab their food and head off to save the arch or stop it from doing any more harm.

THE SYRUP SPILL

The delivery was set to
come a week after
Halloween this year.

8. the syrup spill

Syrup is the perfect addition to ensure that your breakfast will turn from good to great. Glenndale is surrounded by plenty of trees, no doubt a clear source of sap, but they get their syrup from Vermont. They usually come in a truck. A large tank that delivers to a small warehouse on the outskirts of town to package into bottles. The delivery was set to come a week after Halloween this year.

It was a busy day in town. No particular festival celebrating the arrival of syrup. It's just a generally busy day for all of these people, and a few weeks before Thanksgiving.

It was a weekend, the sun was out, but it was still chilly. This is the kind of weather where you want to stay home and eat some pancakes.

❀ ❀ ❀

"I could go for some pancakes." She says into her phone, looking outside her window.

"Want me to come over and make you some?" He asks.

"No, I have to get ready for work."

"Well, what if you didn't show up?"

"The whole place would collapse into chaos, I'm sure," she smiles at the thought.

"Don't you get tired of it, having to take all that responsibility when someone should share the weight with you?"

"You wanna work there with me?" She jokes.

"I could never do what you do and still be polite. You do it so well," he says honestly.

She laughs into the phone.

"Run away with me," he says after a beat.

"Where would we go?" She plays along.

"Anywhere you want to go," he says.

She feels like he means it.

"Oh, you're serious?"

"Very."

She pulls her phone away. She didn't want to nosedive into the deep end. She knows better, should know better, but she hesitates. He makes her happy, makes her smile, and maybe her time in this town has been dragging on for too long.

"What about your job?" She questions.

"I've been relieved of my duties. I have nothing holding me back."

"Um, can I get some time to think?" She says stalling, though her heart knows the answer.

"Of course," he says.

They exchange goodbyes.

* * *

This weather is the perfect weather for staying in and being in silence. She's rocking on her porch despite the weather. This fall season has been the best in all her years.

The best since her husband passed. The best she's felt since telling her "friends" off. Certainly the best in a while now that she feels comfortable to just be herself and exist.

She sits back and looks out over the other houses. She sees a kid holding their parent's hands, jumping up and down, excited to go wherever. She smiles a soft, sad smile. She wants that, still wants that after all these years, and thought maybe she couldn't have that. She looks down at the papers her sister sent her today. Maybe she could have that again. She gets up and goes inside to fill out the forms.

"Maybe we'll have waffles," she says down to her cat who greets her inside.

* * *

This is the weather to clear the air and make way for the season of giving, forgiving, and being grateful for what we have.

"Where are you going?"

"I'm going out to the library, is that an issue mom?"

"No honey, it's not. I just wanted to talk

about last night. I hate when we go to bed angry."

"I didn't go to bed mad, just disappointed," she closes her eyes, "mainly in myself. I don't know why I think I can hide anything in my life and have privacy when you practically run it."

"Honey no, I don't wanna run your life. I just want you to be with me and I want to be with you." She looks at her hands, wringing them to stop the tears.

"Mom, mom," she walks back and grabs her mom's hand, "I want to be with you too, but I'm still my own person. I still want my space and freedom."

"I know now, I'm sorry darling. I'm so sorry. I should've given you the letter as soon as I got it."

"It's okay, I understand, and I'll tell you next time something major happens. No more secrets," she says, hugging her mom briefly.

"You haven't hugged me in months." She sniffles, smiling at her daughter's glowing face.

"I guess we both need it," she says stepping back, "I'll be back soon. Bye, mom."

She walks out the door, texting her friends she'll be at the library soon. At around noon, November 7th, the syrup truck exploded. The contents created huge waves of syrup, killing 17 people and injuring many.

THE MAYOR'S WIFE

"Ladies, how do you feel
about getting into politics?"

9. the mayor's wife

The Mayor of this town, unfortunately, died from a car crash that took not only his life but also the life of Marionette Poloski. And recently as the accident was, just two months ago, there isn't a day when the Mayor's Wife misses him.

She chuckles sadly to herself every time she thinks about it, but sometimes she wishes that he had been an accountant. That he had been a farmer or something not as important as running a town.

After he passed, staff members under her husband stopped by to offer her the position of mayor since she's the wife.

At first, she wanted to kindly decline. Actually, she wanted to tell them to go shove it, but she asked if she could have more time to think. The mayor's wife had no clue what to do, so she did what most women would do in her position. She'd discuss it over with the women in her book club.

It was a unanimous vote that she should take the position. What a powerful statement it would be for their daughters to have a woman as a mayor in their town. The Mayor's Wife doesn't have any kids, so she doesn't know, but these women seem to know and that was enough for her.

They went on about how the male force is too much or how they need more women like her to be an inspiration. They all said they'd be there for her if she needed help.

So with her head held high, the Mayor's Wife accepted the position. Her first act of business was to surround herself with familiarity to help her be the best mayor she could be. She decided that the ladies in her book club would be perfect members of her staff.

* * *

She sits in front of them now to break the news.

"Ladies, how do you feel about getting into politics?" She asks after their daily gossip.

"Women can do all things through the government," Miss Melanie says, "put a woman at the table and a man at her feet and see what happens. That's what I always say." She nods, crossing her arms.

The surrounding women all agree, nodding along.

"Gurl, I second that. We could do some real damage if we were in office let me tell you that," Tanisha's grandma says.

They all go around talking about what they would do if they were in office, all supportive of the rest.

"Why do you ask?" Penelope Harrison peeps out towards the Mayor's Wife.

"Well, I'm glad you asked," she responds, "as you know I accepted the position as mayor."

They all clap again and congratulate her the same as last week.

"Thank you, thank you. I couldn't have done it without y'all, so I was wondering if you would like to be my cabinet members and help me in office." She ends cheerfully.

When around other women it's rude to deny an offer from another woman; especially one you were just a few seconds ago promoting.

All the ladies look at one another. Each looking to see who would be the first one to fold and which would follow her lead. Then Ann Marie stands up. She's the bold one of the group and usually is the one that unknowingly takes the fall for all of them.

"Ladies, weren't we just seconds ago saying what we'd do with this power, sure it isn't a lot but think of your daughters. I have my two boys, and I want to show them that a woman is strong enough and capable enough to help out; especially today. We need representation," she declares.

Ann Marie is also one of the main points of some of the women's topics of gossip; a smaller group dedicated to Ann Marie and her big mouth.

She's loud, unapologetic, and frankly the only thing that gets these women on board in an issue. If none of them step up but Ann Marie does, they'd look like phonies. They all stand up and cheer with her, promising to help the Mayor's Wife and be her cabinet members. All stand and cheer, except for Penelope who tries to quiet the group down. A librarian pops around the corner.

"I'm sorry ladies, could you please lower your voices?" She asks almost as quiet as Penelope.

The Mayor's Wife nods, standing to cross their little circle.

"We're sorry, Darling, we'll keep it down now," she says, all sugary sweet.

The librarian nods her head, then quickly leaves the circle. The women collect themselves and turn to make sure the librarian is gone.

"She really is a pill," Miss Melanie says.

That starts the gossip circle again. They never get to the book they're supposed to read.

THE LIBRARIAN

She never takes a day off,
minus Sundays, but even
then she still hangs around
the library.

10. the librarian

There's only one library in town, and believe it or not, it's a popular hangout spot for kids and adults alike. There are only five librarians on staff.

One of them is ancient and has been there since the library was first built, the other is constantly late to work, two of them never do their jobs, and the last is plain. Although, the plain one is the most dedicated and most focused of the group.

She's not a local and moved here, her choice, about 10 years ago. She wakes up in the morning in her tiny apartment off of Mulberry road and gets ready for work. The Librarian probably understands that she's a plain girl, so to spice up her life she has a collection of over 100 hair ties. On this particular day, she has on a red and black plaid hair bow tie to match her skirt.

She opens up the library every morning at 6 am and closes it at 7 pm. She puts books back, checks late books, and waits for people to slowly trickle in.

The first people to the library are the community college students and a few high school students. She likes to imagine they all have cram sessions and last-minute check-outs for tests.

Next are her employees who know that it doesn't matter if they're late because she'll be there early. The one that's always late shows up three hours later than the opening time.

The next crowd is the parents with their young kids hoping to get them to read a good book. Those kids usually flock around the computers like moths to a flame. The efforts, though appreciated, are lost.

There's another crowd that always sneaks in with the parents and is the group the Librarian is always looking out for. That would be the book club. They come in every day around 10:30 like clockwork. That's when she makes her rounds. It's also where they have their meetings as a cabinet for the mayor's wife's seat in office. She takes the cart of extra books that she sets aside to explore the library and hopes to bump into them.

She turns the corner to their little nook. She stops when she spots a large man surrounding their group huddle. She tries to backtrack, but he spots her. The large man makes his way over to her, so she tries to shrink in size and hide behind a book she has on chewing gum. He looks like he wants to spit her out like chewing gum.

"Can I help you, Miss?" He grumbles out.

"Um..., I'm sorry. I was just trying to...," she trails off.

This man has at least a foot on her and his eyes are gray like a storm. Though she's sure he won't do anything to her, his presence is enough to make her involuntary shrink in size.

"Trying to do what?" He leans towards her, making his bulk more pronounced.

"I'm a librarian. I was just putting this book back on the shelf."

She holds up her little shield for him to see and shakily grabs her name tag to show. He takes both the name tag and the book she was holding.

"Hmm, a book about Chewing Gum?" He asks suspiciously.

"Uh, yep," she squeaks out.

He hands her the book.

"Carry on then."

She takes the book and looks for where it goes. At this point she can't even focus, so she puts it back in the general area and tells herself that she'll fix it later when he leaves. She spins to grab the cart and get the H-E-double hockey stick out of there.

"Hey." The man calls out.

She turns around to face him, her back presses against the cart for support.

"You must be pretty chummy at your job," he picks up the book, "This goes next to the artistry of chewing gum, same author." He places the book in its correct place.

He cracks a half-hearted, one-sided smile at her. She blinks a couple of times just to be sure that he wasn't joking with her. She straightens up and walks back over to him. If there is one thing that you can piss this librarian off about, is telling her that she's doing a crappy job. She walks over to him and looks him dead in the eyes.

"Let's get one thing straight. I am the best librarian this library has ever had. Don't you ever doubt it, and I couldn't focus cause you were scaring me. I was gonna go back and fix it, but thank you for doing it now. So...so good day to you." The Librarian points, losing her steam as he stares down at her.

Turning around, the Librarian grabs the cart and pushes it out and onto the next aisle. Finally breathing out and gripping the cart like it's a lifesaver.

THE BODY GUARD

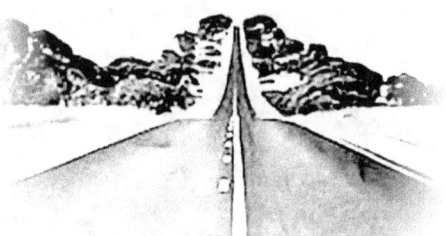

"Ma'am, I'm supposed to be here to protect you," he says.

11. the bodyguard

Rarely do people come to Glenndale for a job, but this man was requested to come and guard a very important lady.

The Bodyguard has worked for very important people before. Some are so important that by exposing their names, he would have to be terminated.

When asked to move to Glenndale to guard a politician, he accepted with no hesitation. He had no permanent home, just a trailer truck on the outskirts of his town. So when he moved, he traded his trailer for a small house near Mulberry Road. The next morning, he went into town hall for his first day of work.

Everyone must have thought this man was some Greek god by the way they were all staring at him, but he was used to it. He suspected that these country folk had never really seen a man with tattoos. Ignoring the stares, he met with the woman he would be protecting.

The Mayor's Wife, or widow of the mayor, was small, with blond hair, and in her late 40's. When they shook hands, she looked a bit flustered and forgot her whole speech about his job.

He was escorted into a room full of more

flustered, middle-aged women. They were giggling around him like school girls at a football pep rally. He kept quiet and listened to instructions. The Mayor's Wife, who he now knows as Ms. Glenndale, explained from her desk what his job would be. Afterward, his first act of business was to study the map of Glenndale and look for possible escape routes.

In other words, he was given busy work. He understood that these women had no idea what they were doing and had little to no knowledge of politics. He should've quit right there, but he was getting paid to do the bare minimum.

From that point on, he became a glorified butler. He would drive Ms. Glenndale around, get her groceries if a storm was too bad, and after a week of that, he would now escort her for her meetings.

He wanted to point out that her being in a public place would draw attention to them, but it seems that she knew that. He caught his first wanderer the other day. A librarian. She was small and timid, with a plaid hair tie to match her skirt. She wasn't a threat, but he looks out for her every time they come to the library.

It's raining today, so all the women scurry ahead of him to avoid getting their hair wet. Safely in their corner, the women all turn to the bodyguard.

"Would you be a dear and get us some coffee please?" Says Ms. Glenndale.

"Ma'am, I'm supposed to be here to protect you," he says.

"We'll be fine, it's not like we'll be mugged," says a woman, who he found out to be named Miss Melanie.

He didn't want to point out how protecting them was his entire job description, but he needed to get away from these women.

They each write down their orders and before he was even five feet away from them did they start talking about him. He made his way over towards the back of the library near the kid's corner. There was a coffee cart that one of the librarians took over. He smiles when he sees that the librarian who chewed him out before is here.

"Good morning," he says softly. His attempt anyways.

The librarian looks up after a while when she decides to set her face in a hard look. An attempt anyways.

"Good morning," she says back, crossing her arms.

He tries to hide his smile at her attempting to be tough. He hands her the paper with the orders and she gets to work. The Bodyguard can't help but notice her precision, and how nimble she is. She gets the first drink done in under a minute.

"You're avoiding me," he says to strike up a conversation.

An odd way to strike up a conversation. She falters for a second then focuses on getting the next drink done.

"I'm not avoiding you," she says, finishing the next drink and moving on, "I was scheduled to work the cart this week."

"That's too bad."

"Why is that?"

"You're the first person to interest me in this town."

She looks down at the cup for some time. Did he upset her?

"Oh, I didn't mean it like that, this town has its perks and all." He tries to correct himself.

It didn't dawn on him that the Librarian could be a native of Glenndale.

"No, no. I'm not from here if that's what you're thinking." She smiles down at the coffee she's finishing.

He nearly sighs out in relief.

"It's just, you said that I'm the first interesting person in this town that you've met." She finishes.

"Oh. Well, you are the first person to talk to me, instead of at me or about me."

A moment passes between them again as she finishes the last cup of coffee.

"Here you go," she looks away to set them all in a tray.

"Thanks." He notices the extra cup.

"It's a peppermint-flavored coffee, to keep you up," she says looking at her hands.

"Thank you." He takes the drinks, leaving

her behind.

He drinks the coffee even though he isn't a fan of sugary things. He takes it anyway and will drink it all just to make conversation again.

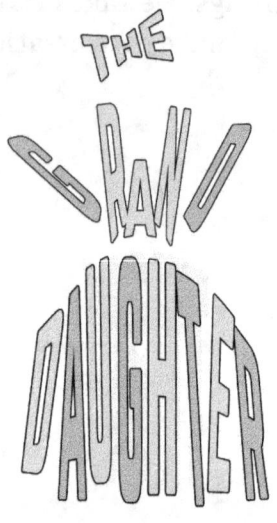

THE GRANDDAUGHTER

Though everyone,
sometimes to her face, calls
her the Granddaughter,
she has a name.

12. the granddaughter

Since it's a small town, the chances are high for everyone to know about everybody's business. And, don't know when to mind their own. The Granddaughter, as she has been called lately, is no stranger to having her own private life put into the business of everyone else in town.

Though everyone, even sometimes to her face, calls her the Granddaughter, she has a name. But her name doesn't matter to others, because before she was the Granddaughter, she was the Daughter.

The Daughter of the town drunk who bought and hoarded all of the town's pineapples. The Daughter that everyone took pity on when her mother left her. Her mother was later found passed out surrounded by at least two weeks worth of Chinese takeout in the library basement. She would earn the title of the Granddaughter later on. The Granddaughter of the woman who wasn't quite as bad as her mom, but was still talked about because she's the town gossip.

In her last year of high school, just as the Granddaughter thought that her life couldn't get more humiliating, her grandma got into politics. Her opinions could be known more than ever.

The Granddaughter was still able to make friends. Though, they all come and go depending on how big of a rumor was spread in town about her life. The one group of friends that she has been with since the beginning of her junior year was a smaller version of her grandma's club.

Instead, it started out as a study group, and then slowly turned into an "Our moms are in Politics club". She didn't want to point out that it was her grandma that was in politics, but she didn't think it was necessary to bring it up. Plus, "Our moms and Grandma are in Politics club" doesn't have a nice ring to it. They all meet up at the library after their parent's and grandma's meeting is over. They basically rant and laugh over what their lives are like. It's fun and she finally feels as if she's found some people that don't take pity on her or judge her based on her past.

She mainly goes through school and pretty much life with her head down and out of everyone's way. Sometimes though, she likes to be on the outside looking in, and the one person she wishes she was more in tune with is her crush.

He also has a name and she knows it too, but sometimes she likes to imagine that he secretly likes her and they don't know each other. That they would be the two perfect strangers destined to meet one another and fall in love.

That can't be it though; that could never happen because they've grown up together. They don't know each other like that, but they went to the same schools, were part of the mandatory chorus class, and even had the same babysitters growing up. Things changed though, and their reputations represent and precede them; especially in her case.

He'll never like the Granddaughter or even know about her besides the kid who went a whole day with gum stuck in her hair. And the girl whose mom would scare all the kids on the way to pick her up from school. The Granddaughter could never be invisible no matter how hard she tried. Her senior year was just starting and now there's definitely no way she could.

"She is seriously starting to give me the biggest migraine." Vivian says, leaning across the couch and putting her legs up on one of the twin's legs.

"What did she do today?" Morgan asks.

She's sitting next to the Granddaughter, leaning her head on her shoulder.

"Ugh, what didn't she do? Tell me that I need to be more feminine or whatever and then."

Vivian sits up straighter and leans into everyone in the group.

"And then she had the audacity to tell me that being a writer doesn't pay the bills." Vivian finishes.

"I guess she hasn't heard of Stephen King, huh?" The Granddaughter comments.

"God, I want to be better than King, though that man is a straight-up legend. I'd give my firstborn to meet him." Vivian flops back.

"And you will one day. I'm still thinking about that story with the scarecrow you told."

Morgan shudders a little about the night of scary stories. The Granddaughter pops up.

"I'm gonna get some water, be back."

She rounds their section and makes a beeline towards the water fountains. On her way back, she spots a book. She turns back, making a grab for it but the book comes through on the other side. She rounds the corner to see who it is and stops dead in her tracks. It's the crush, and today he's looking particularly handsome. He looks up and notices her.

"Sorry, were you going for this book too?" He asks.

"Uh, no, no. You touched it first, so it's all yours."

She's hoping that would be the end of the conversation, but he's persistent.

"No, ladies first." He extends the book out to her.

She looks around for an exit, an excuse, a sinkhole to swallow her whole. Then, she notices that there is another copy of the book.

"Uh." She reaches for the next book and shows it to him.

He laughs.

"Well I guess now we can both read it."

"Yea, and maybe start a mini book club," she blurts out to make conversation. Why would she do that? Of all the days to be chatty, she thinks.

"Hmm, maybe," he smiles, turning to leave, "Well, I'll see you around, Tanisha."

She watches him leave, her heart pounding so hard against her chest. Her name. He knows her name.

Watch out boys, she'll chew
you up.

13. the man-eater

She's a homewrecker, a flirt, a man-eater. Watch out boys, she'll chew you up. She has developed quite the reputation without even moving a finger, and she took force in high school.

Senior boys really wanted her, so she got invited to all the parties. She went to prom her freshman year and even had two serious boyfriends all within that year.

Then one day, word got around that she had slept with four guys in one week. Kenneth Wheeler High School would never look at her the same. Not like they respected her much before, but now they have more proof and an excuse.

The problem that stands is that she wasn't any of those things. Sure, she went to prom her freshman year. She even thought that he had loved her, but she left that night early, getting ice cream with her dad instead.

The other boyfriend was in her grade, but he also wasn't a keeper. She was aware of what she had become ever since seventh grade, and frankly, she was proud of herself and her body. But people can easily mistake confidence with arrogance. People didn't get her, she never made friends in middle or high school. Well, that's not all true, as her only real friends were guys.

She felt more comfortable in their presence. They were honest, brutally honest, but she'd take it over gossip and the backstabbing of girls.

She hadn't slept with four guys; she's actually never lost her virginity. She was assigned to a group project with four guys and one other girl. The guys and Jackie were goofing off and having fun. The other girl must've taken it as a threat and texted everyone she knew that little Jackie Oak took it upon herself to give these guys what they wanted.

Shortly after, Jackie was blacklisted from the school and she lost the few girl friends she had.

She couldn't explain herself, she never could, because it's who she is. She has friends that are boys, she loves her body, and she's never had to explain herself to anyone before. One girl who dated one of the guys in the group went as far as to call her out and say that she is the reason that they broke up.

A homewrecker. That's what they called her for weeks. But she would never let them see her with her head down. She would sit alone at lunch, and in class she'd only answer if called on. When she got home, she'd go to her room and cry.

She couldn't go to her father, he'd already had enough on his plate and wouldn't need her teenage drama. So she'd cry until her head started to hurt, make dinner, and wait for him to get home. They'd eat and she'd lie about her day, then they'd go to their own rooms. She'd always glance over at the letter opener resting on the desk in the soft glow of her lamp.

It was her mother's. She gave it to her one Christmas; and though Jackie would never get letters, she'd always keep it near her.

The only thing her mother left her with. Jackie would always look at it before going to bed. Sometimes she'd just pull it out and look it over. It was golden and heavy.

She'd press it against her arm just to feel the weight. Then she'd put it away and turn the lights off. Staring up at her ceiling telling herself over and over again. Writing it all over her mind as she drifted off to sleep.

"I am not a homewrecker. I am not a homewrecker."

THE BLIND MAN

Being both lonely and blind,
he would search for
someone to keep him
company.

14. the blind man

"My my. Don't you look dashing, who are you trying to impress?" The Blind Man's caretaker teases.

"An angel, but I'm afraid that I'll still look under-dressed next to her," he says, straightening his tie.

His caretaker smooths the crinkles on his jacket. She's helping him get ready for the vet's ball at the retirement home. Like most men at his age, he served his time in the military. Served during Vietnam, as a matter of fact. It wasn't the war that made him blind, but something in his family line that finally caught up with him. He was only twenty when he enlisted, and afterwards, he never married, had no kids, but all he had was one lover before the war. Well, secret love anyways.

They were best friends growing up, but once he got back wanting to tell her how he really felt. She was gone. It took him some time to find out that she had moved away to a small town he didn't know. He went about his life hoping maybe to forget her.

Being both lonely and blind, he would search for someone to keep him company. He had a good therapy dog that kept him company for almost twenty years. He had a few girlfriends, but they come and go. He was an only child growing up, so no siblings, nieces, or nephews to keep him company. He lost all feeling in his legs about two years ago, another thing that his family passed to him. He decided that it was best for his neighbors and his emotional health that he admit himself into a home.

It was the best decision he's ever made. He had a few friends, good food, and a caretaker who he thought of as his own child. Yet, he still felt this feeling of darkness overcoming him. It followed him ever since the war, perhaps even before when he grew up with only one friend. He was in the Glenndale retirement home when he decided to look up his old friend and love after almost fifty years. She was also here in Glenndale, just down the street.

"Well, you still look sharp," she says, saluting him. She grabs his hand to salute her back. He laughs.

She wheels him off to the ballroom where all the other veterans wait.

"Do you think she found this place alright?" He asks, fiddling with his tie.

"I'm sure she found this place just fine," she says, patting his shoulder gently, "I see her over there."

"Can you describe her to me please?" He says, grabbing at her hand.

"Oh, she's beautiful. She has on a baby blue

dress, silky smooth with silver glitter. Her silver kitten heels and earrings match. Her hair is curled around the ends, her makeup is light with red lips and her world-famous cat-eyed glasses." She laughs at the last part.

He smiles softly as his caretaker waves a hand towards her to get her attention. She spots them, walking over.

"Hello," she says shyly to the Blind Man.

"Hello," he says back, just as shy.

The woman turns to the caretaker for a hug. "Hello dear."

"You two have seen each other more than enough times to not be shy around each other anymore." The Caretaker squeezes her back and looks at him too.

"I'm sorry if I'm taken aback. It's just that you described the most beautiful woman in the world and I'm a bit unprepared." He says, rubbing the back of his neck.

"Oh stop, silly goose. Care to dance?" She asks, grabbing his hand.

"Anything for you, my sweet Lucinda," he says as she pushes him out to the dance floor.

The caretaker sits back and looks at the scene before her. How she wishes for that kind of love. She sighs as the couple smile at one another as if they're the only ones on planet earth.

THE COUNCIL MEMBERS

No one willingly moves to
Glenndale.

15. the council members

When a kid leaves Glenndale, usually for school, a majority of them never show their faces back again. Never again, unless they absolutely have to.

They visit their parents, take them out for dinner, and then leave only to return for the next holiday. Those who do return on their own account are either back for jobs or money.

Everyone in town can tell who those kids are. Maybe they were a problem growing up, skipping town early just to leave, and only to return years later when life doesn't cut it as a yoga instructor. They're the kind to emerge from their parent's home to do the chores or pick up dad's medication.

One might try not to look at them, but it's hard to ignore when they vowed never to return, only to be at your office waiting for an interview.

There are a few who are requested to come here for their services. No one willingly moves to Glenndale. Either you were born here or you were called to be here. The two council members were requested to come in to work a position in town.

"The Mayor's Wife has a job for us, this better be good," one council member says to the other.

He was born in Glenndale. He first went to college in-state, then went the extra mile to get more of his studies done in a college out of state. He was doing well until he was laid off about a year ago. He refused to come back to town if that meant being one of those people. He decided to look for more positions, but until then he worked at a local bookstore in his new town.

He received a call from one of his friends saying there was a position in Glenndale for council members.

This was some sort of loophole because he would be going back with a job. Swallowing his pride, he accepted the job and purchased an apartment as far away from his parent's as he could get.

"She's not the Mayor's wife anymore, she's just the mayor." The other councilwoman scolds.

She was also born in Glenndale. They both went to school together, grew up together. They were actual neighbors before she moved out.

She took a different route and decided to study law in Massachusetts. She was a good lawyer who won a majority of her cases. But the issue was that her employer was less than honest with his methods of owning a law firm. She and her fellow employees were given their last paychecks while their boss was carried to prison.

She refused to be one of those people who asked their parents for help or even return to

Glenndale unless she needed to take care of her mom.

She worked at a smaller firm and was given busy work more than often, but it kept her sane.

She received a call from the secretary of the mayor asking her about a position as the mayor's council member. She thought of this loophole. She'd come back with a job and take care of her mom if anyone asked. She accepted, asked her mom for her old room back, and moved back into town.

"Yea yea, but what are her intentions? According to Janine, she already fired two groups of council members and we're the third."

"Gee thanks. I know how to count," she replies back as they climb the stairs to the town hall.

"All I'm saying is that I already have an idea on her and I can't afford to lose this job," he says.

"Believe me, I know. I can't lose this job either, but we have to put our faith in her. Plus, based on my talk with her on the phone, she sounds like a competent woman."

"Woman telepathy," he mumbles under his breath.

She bumps him and slips in when he holds the door open for her to the meeting room. A few members were already there. No one is familiar to them besides each other. They sit next to one another and shake hands with the other members, just as the door opens and the mayor's wife walks in.

"Alright everybody, take your seats and let's get started," she says enthusiastically.

The two council members look at each other, then turn to the mayor. Perhaps this might be tougher than they thought.

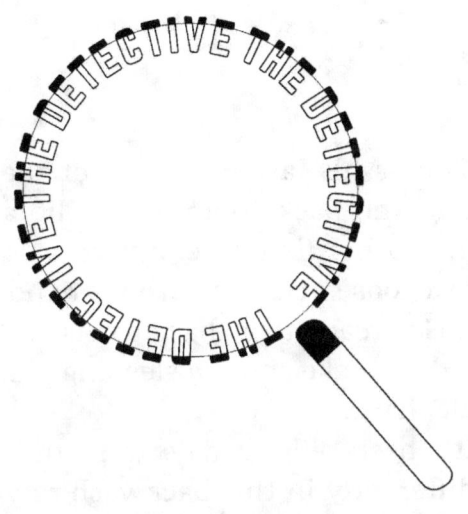

He got to the town at around
noon, expecting a case of
kidnapping or even murder...

16. the detective

This is his last interview of the day. He's waiting in the back room of the library, where according to his first interviewee was when all "hell broke loose." He sits with his hands covering his face. He's ready to go back to his not so crappy motel bed and take enough sleeping pills to knock out an elephant.

It's been a long day. It seems that time works differently in this backwash town. He was called the day of the incident if you can even call it that. Not the accident that took the lives of 17 people, but the one where the librarian goes missing. He got to the town at around noon, expecting a case of kidnapping or even murder, but he felt like his time is being wasted.

Her apartment was full of her stuff, no signs of forced entry, struggle, and nothing out of the ordinary was taken. It seems that she had cats and they were missing, but that wasn't anything to sneeze about. Some jewelry and other expensive items were still there. The Tv, computer, even some pills are all in their place.

He chalked it up to her leaving on vacation.

The first person he interviewed gave him nothing but his second headache of the day.

"She always shows up bright and early to open the library. She never takes days off and she's always there before me and my other employees to help set up."

"Ma'am," he said, taking a gentle sip of his seltzer water, "I don't mean to play this off as nothing. She could've taken a well-deserved and needed sick day or a vacation, don't you think?"

"But she would've told someone. She would've told me." The woman had wrung and tore her tissue to shreds.

"Are you her boss?"

"Well, no." She sniffled

"Does she manage the library?" He asked slowly.

"Yes."

"Have you taken sick days off?"

"Yes, I have."

"Well, thank you for your time, could you bring in the next person?"

She got up, pushed her chair in, and left. He took his time to let out a long groan.

The next people are her fellow employees and all basically say the same thing. She never takes sick days, basically runs the place, and has been taking this crap for ten years. He takes the notes, but he knows what this is.

He hears the door open now as he finishes up a doodle of a bird.

"Come in and close the door please," he says, tossing the notebook down, knocking back his water with his third aspirin.

A girl comes in and sits down. He starts to bring his phone out to record, but he can't even bring himself to do that.

"Alright. My name is Detective— "

"Aren't you gonna record this?" She cuts him off.

He leans forward.

"Listen, kid. I can already tell you what this is. I don't need your statement, but the thought of an odd number of interviews makes me sick." He gives a fake smile.

"You really aren't gonna take this seriously?" She asks, crossing her arms.

"Nope, 'cause what half of this town explained to me sounds like a classic case of I-need-to-get-the-hell-out-of-this-place-itis. She just caught on before she got trapped."

She gives him a look before laughing.

"Oh my gosh. This whole hard-boiled detective act is so cliche," she laughs some more before quieting down, "you really don't know anything, do you?"

"I guess not," he says. Grinding his teeth, slowly loses his patience.

"You don't know the first thing about us or what we go through every day. Our world is a petri dish and you all are on the outside looking in on us like we're bacteria. Like we're some foreign creature.

We lost so many lives today, a few kids

came back from the dead, and now a woman goes missing and you don't even bother to check?" She asks, not trying hard enough to lose her patience.

"She has a boyfriend, and it's a small town. You eventually find out about people on your own. We got nothing on him. Do you?" She continues, pointing at him, "now he seems like a nice guy and all, and maybe it's just nothing. But, you don't get to treat us like we're idiots when it could be something major." She says finally, getting up and storming out.

He looks at the door. The boyfriend. Children missing, and unexplained sightings. Maybe he misjudged this town and what's really going on. His third headache of the day, finding out what this town is about.

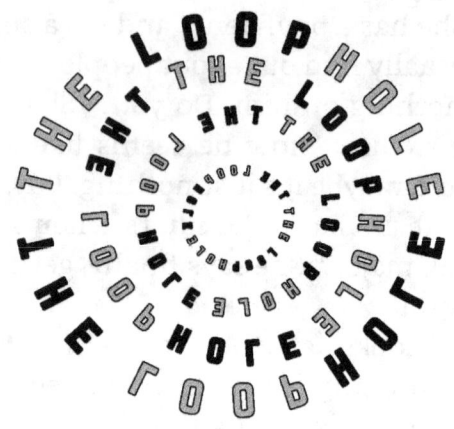

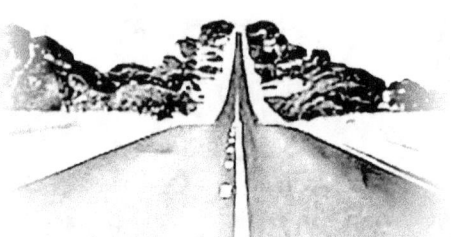

"Wait a second," she says,
looking around, "we've done
this before."

17. the loophole

Strange things happen in the woods. Strange things happen in Glenndale altogether, but rarely do strange things happen to all of the people at the same time.

Rarely does a phenomenon happen to a whole town. Then again, Glenndale is always the exception.

Everyone's heard of Groundhog's day, right?

The idea that some strange occurrence out of the ordinary can cause a skip in time. It makes more sense that this could happen to one person, and they alone have to figure out why it's happening to them.

But how does a town of entirely different people figure it out?

* * *

"Wait a second," she says, looking around, "we've done this before."

He looks around too. They have done this before. Sure they would sneak off to the woods as kids, but this was different. They were just here.

"Like Déjà vu," he whispers.

She looks at him, shaking her head.

"What time is it?"

"It's noon."

"What day?"

"November 7th," he says.

They share a horrified look and start heading back out of the woods.

"What did we do next?" He asks, trying his best to hide the waver in his voice.

"We were heading back to the car, and something caused me to fall."

"The explosion."

That's right. There was a loud bang and it seemed as if there was an earthquake.

They were coming up to the arch.

"Let's go around it," he says slowly as if trying to remember if that's the thing that he said before.

"Yea." She agrees.

They both steadily walk around it. Then turn back to look at it.

"Maybe it was a fluke, maybe—"

She's cut off as an explosion and a rumble sends them backward. She passes right under the arch.

* * *

"What the hell?" Tanisha looks around.

"What's going on guys? We've done this

three times it feels like," Morgan says.

The girl next to her looks around. She points.

"Look, over there is a guy who trips, but plays it off as if he's tying his shoes," they all look and sure enough he does.

"What's going on, this can't be déjà vu," one of the twins says.

They all look up the stairs.

"Behind those doors is chaos, right?" Vivian asks, "is it just us who's stuck?"

"But that's not how it works, how can all of us experience this all at the same time?" Tanisha asks, a horrified look passes behind her glasses.

They all cautiously climb the stairs and push the doors to the library open. The chaos is a little bit quieter. Everyone looks around confused; like they've been here before.

"What the hell is going on?" A man yells at the older librarian.

"Back off dude, we're all just as confused." Vivian pushes him aside to speak to the older woman.

"We've done this before. I've done this before," she says, looking near to a heart attack, "Ellie's gone. I don't know where, but I wonder if she understands what's going on. Maybe she left town."

She picks up the phone and dials her number. The group looks at each other.

"Isn't there an explosion?" The other twin

asks cautiously.

Just like that, a loud boom that rocks against the library. People screaming and pushing. Then everything goes black in the room.

❋ ❋ ❋

"Ian, honey, just calm down," she tries to comfort him, but he paces away.

"Stay calm," he walks over to her, "we have tried to leave this town like ten times. How many times do we always die just at the edge of town? Right before we hit the sign and start over again?" he asks, "and no matter how much gas we take or get an early start. We always die, right here on this road?"

"I don't know. I don't know, okay. It's not just us though. Regina called me back from the library a few times, it's happening to the whole town."

"That doesn't make it better. We're stuck here. Stuck in this loop. Stuck repeating the same stuff, just different variations of it." He says, resting on the hood of the car.

A sad look passes over her face. Walking over and joining him on the hood. Sitting next to him, her jacket wrapped tightly around her.

"There's no one I'd rather be stuck in a loop with than you. Even if we die a thousand times, I'm glad it's you," she leans into him.

He holds her tight. Then pulls her into him, just as the truck screeches, flips, then explodes.

It's been November 7th for some time now. It's been a little past noon that the truck skids then explodes. They're caught in a loop, and none of them know how to get out.

"Aw come on Chris. It's still early. Let's go for some coffee, huh?"

18. coffee and blood

"Sorry, we're closed," a man says from behind his newspaper.

"I wanna look at your selection quickly, got any caps?" Another man says back.

The man looks up past his paper. A guy in a trench coat covered in droplets and a fedora pushed over his face greets him at the counter.

"I think we got something in the back," he says, setting down his paper.

He picks up his son from the chair next to him, carrying him off to his office to his other son.

"Take your brother home."

"What about you?"

His son looks so much like him now, and smarter than him when he was his age. He probably knows all the bad things his Daddy's ever done. He probably will never come back home the minute he turns eighteen. His son stares back at him now in question.

"I'll be home shortly," the man says finally.

His son doesn't nod or anything as he carries his brother in his arms and takes him out of the office.

The man watches his sons go until they

disappear behind the corner. He locks the front doors, turns off his office lights, then heads to the back. Down some stairs and to the left is his other office. He holds the door for the man, then sits behind his desk.

"I got a message from Harry." The man in his trench coat says, taking off his hat.

"Harry too much of a sissy to tell me himself?" The man responds, crossing his arms.

"He's got a lot on his plate, and so do I, but I was in the neighborhood."

The men stare at each other.

"Whatever, what did he want to tell me?" He sits back in his chair.

"He says he's out."

"Out?" he says back.

"Yea, he's out."

"Hmm." The man rubs his chin.

"That's all you gotta say? No number of yours, no fury, no cursing our family name with your Italian crap?"

The man laughs.

"No, nothing like that. Sure, I'm pissed, 'cause I'm getting screwed over, but I understand."

"You do?" He asks, one eyebrow raised.

"Chris, I'm a father. You think I really want this life for my boys?" He sits forward in his chair, "It's a minor setback, but all's well."

"Well, that's good." Chris breathes out slowly.

"Yea. Anything else Chris, or we done here?"

"Well, he also wanted to know about the dough." Chris tests the waters of the man's patience, but not meeting the man's eyes.

"The dough?" He parrots, his eyebrows raised now.

"Yea, wants to know where it is?" Chris asks, looking at his fingernails instead.

The man clicks his teeth as if to think for a second. Chris fidgeting his legs in response.

"He asked that?" He asks finally.

"Yep." Chris stops shaking his leg but scratches his head instead.

"Hmm, so not only is your brother screwing me over, but he's asking personally where the money is? The ones that I'd give to those who work with me, huh?"

"Ahh, Paul it's nothing like that. It's just bad timing. Our ma's not doing so well. He just wants to take a break for a while, that's all."

"Which is it? He's taking a break or he wants out?" Paul asks.

They go silent.

"Listen, man, I'm giving you a hard time," Paul says, leaning back, "I understand, you don't gotta make excuses on my account. He wants out, fine by me. He wants to know where the dough is. I can't do that. You know that Chrissy. So tell him that if he wants out, he has my blessing." He says, clapping and standing up, "Alright?"

"Yea," Chris says, standing up too, and heading out the office in a hurry, "well, uh goodnight Paul. Blessings to your family."

"Aw come on Chris. It's still early. Let's go for some coffee, huh?" He says, putting on his trench coat.

He looks towards the door. They head out and lock up.

"Be sure to get that message across to your brother, huh?" Paul claps Chris on the back.

"Sure thing," Chris says.

* * *

Chris was later found dead at the diner. And the money that was the share of Harry still hasn't been recovered.

Both sons of Paul believe it's somewhere in the store, but they've each given up that part of themselves. The oldest refuses to talk to his dad and the youngest can't get anything out of his dad anymore. They sold the place to this other guy who wants a hat store.

Probably a front for some other crap.

FLASHLIGHT TAG

One game they all loved to play late at night is flashlight tag.

19. flashlight tag

The summer before the blue moon film festival was one of a spectacle.

It was summer before everything went wrong, but it was a summer to remember. There were fireworks, popsicles, picnics, and late-night dips in the pool.

The people of Glenndale love summer as much as they love making up random holidays to celebrate.

Even the kids have fun away from their computers and phones.

All outside, even past 9 o'clock. They would run out behind the school or out in the fields next to the woods. Never venturing in though.

They would play red rover, red light, green light, and hide and seek. But one game they all loved to play late at night is flashlight tag.

The game is like tag, but instead of your hands to tag people, it's a flashlight. If you're tagged, you go to jail, which is usually a tree stump or lamppost. There's usually a guard watching the prisoners. If the guard is tagged by someone else then it's an automatic jailbreak.

There's another version of this game. It's called frantic mode.

A sort of last-man-standing game. Where anyone can tag anyone and whoever is left wins.

This particular night, the kids decided to play frantic mode. The game works best with a lot of kids. And you can form alliances, but in the end, though it wouldn't matter as much.

Tonight, there were sixteen kids. This includes the one older kid, an eighth-grader to make sure all the kids came back home.

They all run away before turning on their flashlights. Then after a five-second countdown, the game begins.

Once you're tagged, you have to turn your flashlight up to the sky and wave it around like a watchtower. Once you get to the older kid, you turn it off, sit near them until that round is over and a new round starts again.

The games tend to go by quickly as kids join alliances, take out the other kids only to then turn on themselves.

The teams have an odd number, but a kid sits out every once in a while to catch her breath. She has asthma, but it doesn't stop her from playing unless the older kid tells her to take a breather.

Her asthma isn't as bad this time, but she sits out this round.

It's dark outside minus the stars and the flashlights. All the kids can't see each other, but they know someone is sitting next to them. They can tell by an outline and the rustle of the grass next to them. The only real glow close to them is the older kid's phone.

He gets up to take a call as a new round starts. They all go, some lasting longer than others. The girl with asthma sits down next to the older kid's chair. She notices that someone is sitting in it real quiet. The teen comes back.

So, the kid gets up and sits down next to her.

"I lost my flashlight," he says.

"I can help you look for it," she offers, getting up.

She turns on her flashlight, careful not to shine it in his face. They walk out onto the field, sweeping the ground for his flashlight. Kids running past them, a couple shining the light on them.

"Hey dorks, you can't tag the ground."

"Shut up dummy," she says.

"Yea, shut up dummy," the kid next to her mocks back. They run off, laughing with one another.

"Over here," she says, spotting a red flashlight on the ground."

He reaches over to pick it up.

"Thank you," he says.

He turns it on then points it up to the sky. She does the same. He starts to laugh, running around making noises as she does the same. They both fall onto the ground laughing.

"Hey kids," the teen shouts, "let's go, gotta

get home."

They get up and run over to line up with the other kids.

"Line up. Hey. Don't point," he says to a kid shining the light in his face, "actually lineup and lights off."

They all obey and turn their lights off.

"Alright," he touches each of their heads and counts. The girl with asthma and the kid at the end giggle more as he gets closer.

"Fourteen, fifteen, and I make sixteen. Alright, let's go," he says, shining his flashlight on them as they all march home.

She never did see the kid's face.

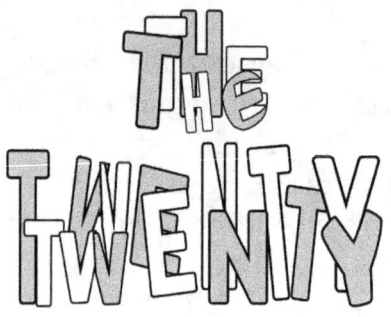

THE TWENTY

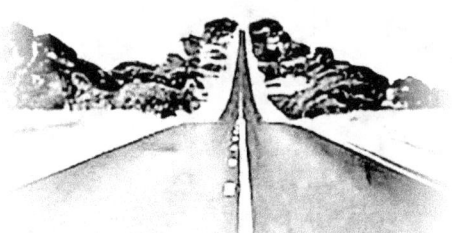

About 10 years ago, twenty students and their teacher went missing.

20. the twenty

About 10 years ago, twenty students and their teacher went missing. They had left for a camping trip, but then never came back. Parents, the county police, and everyone in the town searched the entire woods. They even checked the campsite hoping to find anything about their kids.

For a month they searched and searched, but after no clue to where they could be, they stopped looking.

Memorials were put up and a plaque was dedicated to each of the parents for their kids. The twenty's disappearance was honored on the day they went missing.

Then one day, on the day the kids were supposed to come back from their trip, a bus passed back through the arch.

It was about four in the afternoon, and the school bus that they left on came rolling through town.

The bus was the same, but it was covered in soot and caked in years of dirt. Some of the windows cracked, but you could see that the kids were all in their seats.

The whole town followed the bus back to the school. There were no doors on the bus and when the kids stepped off there was something different about all of them.

They were still the same age when they disappeared, but there was something about their eyes. They looked as if they had been through hell and back.

Parents pushed through, hugging and holding their kids, and crying into their shoulders. Some kids too in shock to react back and other kids completely falling into their parent's arms.

The Mayor's Wife pushed through the crowd and gathered around the children and their parents. She invited them to the town hall for a dinner; a celebration she cried. She had tears in her own eyes, hugging each of the parents and kids. They all agreed as best as they could through their tears and runny noses.

The dinner was set to be in a few days, giving the twenty plenty of time to catch up on current events.

They missed the birth of siblings, graduations, and past elections. They missed it all, but some things didn't seem to matter to them.

They never left their parent's side, which meant that they were home or at work all day.

They ran into siblings who were once younger, but are older than them now. It was bizarre and unsettling, to say the least, but they held them like you would for any lost family member.

When the twenty weren't with their

parents, they were in each other's company. They would just sit in the park and watch as the people went by.

Their blank, but horrified stares gazing upon the crowd who could never understand, and who never would.

Local news teams and papers sought out to interview them, but parents declined and told them to have sympathy.

Around the time of the dinner at the town hall, the kids looked well, they'd been fed, bathed, clothed, and had a bed to sleep in. But through their closed smiles and dull eyes, you could tell that they still had a war bubbling inside of them. The dinner was going well, despite the parents talking for them the entire time. Even if they didn't talk for them, their kids wouldn't have anything to say.

Then a reporter asked the question everyone in the room and the whole town was too afraid to ask.

"Where did you all go, and what did you see?" He asks.

Parents looked on, ready to shout when suddenly a boy with blonde hair combed away from his brown eyes stood up. He looked right at the reporter and the rest of the kids looked at the boy. A girl next to the blonde kid grabbed at his sleeve.

"Honey, please," she says.

"No, he wants to know." He says sternly.

Though he had the voice of a thirteen-year-old boy, it carried authority like a grown man.

"We went camping as planned. We passed through the big arch on our way out, but then we saw planes pass by, and then the bombs dropped."

A few kids shudder, a couple of them start to cry as he continues.

"It landed on the town, this very town. We saw them land all around us. Back on the bus, Mr. Crason told us from the radio that it was like the apocalypse. 10 years we lived off of scraps and hunted for dinner. It was a miracle that we were able to stay together and alive, but we did. Except for Mr. Carson." He trailed off a little.

Some of the kids turned their heads down, wiping at their eyes quickly.

"One day, we all found and rebuilt the big stone arch we passed through, thinking maybe that could be our way back. It was a theory and took us forever to find all the pieces, but it was the only hope we had. We all got on the bus and here we are now, so to answer your question. We saw hell, we lived, and won. So put that in your blog." He says, sitting down hard.

Everyone was silent, then it got hysterical.

The Bodyguard pushed back some of the reporters as the Mayor's Wife tried to dim the situation. Parents pulled kids out and away from the town hall.

Some would later go to therapy, others back to school, but it wouldn't matter. No one would or could ever understand what those kids went through.

And as much as they wished to make their kids happy again, they were too afraid of the answer they'd get.

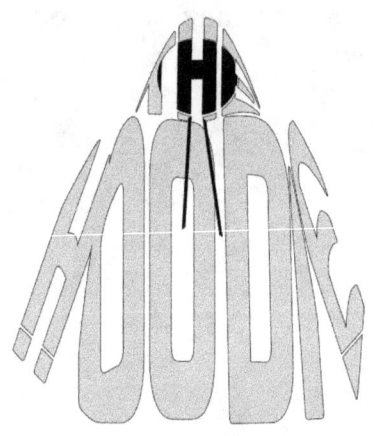

Maybe it's the hoodie giving
her powers, but she isn't
too sure.

21. the hoodie

Marionette Poloski has had a string of bad luck since the age of ten.

Her goldfish jumped out of the bowl and died at age 11. When she got her period at age 13, she was wearing a long white dress. At age 14, her very first kiss eneded with the guy gagging.

And though her mother tried to reassure her saying maybe he knew he was gay before he kissed her, it still didn't help.

And today, the day that she turned 17, someone spilled Gatorade on her top by accident. Red Gatorade and a white top, it seems that she hadn't learned her lesson on wearing white things to school.

She drips down the hallway towards the lost and found in the main office for any type of covering. She pulls out a red hoodie with a green four-leaf clover on it.

"Where have you been all my life?" She mumbles under her breath.

She heads to the bathroom to trade out her top for the hoodie. It's a little big on her, but it'll do.

She throws her shirt in a plastic bag and heads out the door, running straight into someone.

"Oh, I'm sorry," she says, reaching to pick up whoever's books she knocked down. It turns out that it was Roman. The tall, tan, and handsome boy that has made number one on her list of cutest boys ever since they were kids.

"Hey, it's cool. Oh," he says as she stands up.

She suddenly feels self-conscious, pulling herself closer in the hoodie.

"Wow, it's just, um. Can I walk you to class?" He asks, stumbling over his words.

He was fumbling over her. Him, asking her to walk to class. Together. What in the world is going on?

"Uh sure," she says and as they walk to her English class she tries to think.

It's hard to focus with him next to her.

"Well, uh this is me," she says, pointing to the doors as a few people pool in.

"Cool, so I'll see you around." He sticks out his hand.

"Um, Marionette," she says, blushing.

"Roman," he shakes her hand and he gives her that smile that can impregnate girls.

He turns and walks away, but not before turning back.

"Dope hoodie by the way."

She hugs herself tighter and walks into the room. Maybe it's the hoodie giving her powers, but she isn't too sure. One guy talking to her doesn't prove a thing. She needed more proof.

And proof she got.

For about a month, and leading into summer, wherever she took the hoodie good luck followed her.

Roman became her boyfriend and they were able to travel to a lake house together for a week in summer. She won her dream car in a lottery. She came across old money from her family. Better yet, her skin started to clear, so that's all the proof she needs.

She'd wash the hoodie, obviously, but for the first week of research, she didn't. She was afraid that the water would ruin the luck.

Her life was starting to turn out better and it was all thanks to this hoodie. If it was hot, she'd wear it around her waist or put it in her car if she was traveling. She and Roman would use it as a pillow on the night that they laid out under the tree on the hill and shared their first kiss.

She and Roman are at the park now, but in a hurry of being late, she left the hoodie on her desk. She didn't realize it until they were eating.

She heads to her car claiming to forget something. She searches everywhere and can't find it. She had become so dependent on it and now it was gone.

What if not having it causes her and Roman to break up? What if her acne returns? What if those lottery tickets were fake? Returning to Roman she sits down gingerly, looking around for any bad thing that could happen.

"Alright, what's up with you?" He asks jokingly.

"Nothing, um here I forgot the hand sanitizer." She passes him the bottle.

"Cool," he takes some and grabs her hand to wipe it too.

She pulls back as she feels a sting. A cut. Oh God, it's already begun.

"Mari, what's the matter," he pulls her closer, "You look like you were just told your puppy died."

She has to tell him.

"Roman, I'm just scared. What if things go bad in our last year, what if I say something stupid and you leave? What if you don't like me anymore?" She asks into her hands. He lifts her chin.

"Where is this coming from?" He pulls her close to him, resting his chin on her head.

"My life has just been a series of bad luck and I don't want to lose you," she says into his shoulder.

"Hey, this summer, no scratch that. When I first met you and we hung out. I wanted to know more about you. It wasn't luck that brought us together, fate maybe, but also maybe me tackling you in the hall"

She laughs a little.

"Are you sure?"

"I'm positive," he looks at her. "I'm not leaving. I love you," he says confidently.

Her smile starts to grow and grow.

"I love you too," she says, wrapping her arms around his neck.

The weekend before the first day of school was bliss. For three days she didn't wear the hoodie and she started to believe that maybe the hoodie didn't have any powers.

She hung it up and put it back in her closet. She got dressed and headed to her car for school. She pulled up to a stop sign and saw a car come barreling after her that knocked her into traffic. She collided with a car that pulled out from its sign at the same time.

UNDER THE W'MAN STAIRS

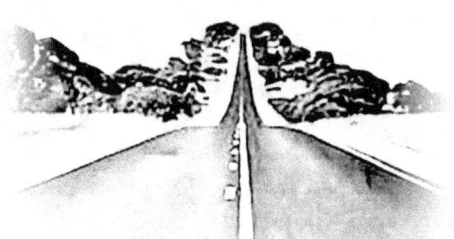

She walked around the little
maze that the woman had
called home.

22. the woman under the stairs

A mom was screaming at the police, turning bright red, and trying to cover herself in her robe.

Her daughter was sitting on the porch. The red and blue lights flashing over her face as someone wraps a blanket around her shoulders.

The new phone she held, lighting up with messages. Probably her friend's. Probably her boyfriend, but she doesn't care right now.

She doesn't care anymore because she's seen enough things in her life to fill up an encyclopedia. So she didn't care that a woman had been living under their stairs for years.

* * *

There is a small exception of people coming to Glenndale to escape the law. It's only happened a couple of times, but even then the criminal lies low then leaves town before anyone notices.

The woman, however, had been living in the backroom in the basement. The one full of storage that goes all the way up to the ceiling.

When the daughter came back, some of the boxes were removed, and though it wasn't enough to give it away. The woman knew her cover was soon to be compromised.

It was the daughter who discovered her at night. It was maybe two weeks after her return. She went down looking for one of her books when she noticed a set of blankets folded over an air mattress. She went in further to investigate.

She saw a few of her books out of their boxes, a mini-fridge, and newspapers. She picked up one of her reading lamps and shined it over the arrangement.

She walked around the little maze that the woman had called home.

* * *

"She was comfortable," the daughter tells the police now, "I noticed that she had a key made. I found it near where she slept," she says, down at the police station.

She can still hear her mom crying in the other room.

"How long do you think she was there?"

"Based on what I found. I say a little after I was gone," she says, sitting back.

She wasn't irritated at her mom for not noticing a stranger in her house. She was a little confused about why the woman got so comfortable.

* * *

She searched more of the back room. She knocked along the walls for the false door. This room used to be her dad's office. He showed it to her when she was younger. Told her it led directly outside.

That was her secret spot for hiding whenever her dad was on the phone. It was big enough for her to crawl through with no trouble. She knocked until she heard a hollow spot. She felt for a handle before pulling it open.

* * *

"I know she got in through the secret door, it leads outside. I don't know how she found it, but it hardly matters now," she says looking over at them, "what was she in for anyways?"

"That's confidential ma'am, we can't release that kind of information." One of the cops says.

"I don't think you understand," she says, leaning forward, "doesn't my privacy matter? Doesn't my mom's privacy matter? She has been living alone in that house for ten long years and that dangerous woman has been right under her doing who knows what. She could've been an active criminal, a serial killer, hell even just a stalker. And you're telling me I can't find out. Why was she there and why so long?!" She shouts.

Then it hit her.

She was gone for ten years. Parents were

grieving, there was chaos everywhere. The woman on the run happened to fall into the right place at the right time.

This woman took advantage of her mother's grief and got comfortable under her stairs.

No one would question or look around a mother's home whose daughter was presumably dead. She got comfortable. Thought she could live like this.

Then they all returned. Once again it was chaotic, but it didn't work in her favor.

She couldn't get out now. Too many people, too many cops. She decided to lay low. Maybe the daughter wouldn't notice her here now that she was back. Unfortunately for the woman, the daughter did notice.

* * *

The daughter crawled through the hidden door until she reached the outside. Just behind the bushes. She crawled up and looked up.

The woman was looking right back at her.

"She was just looking at me. I couldn't read her expression. It was too dark, but I could tell that she didn't know what to do. Ten years of never getting caught, only to one day come back and get caught by a little girl," she chuckles despite herself.

She walks out to meet her mom. Grabbing her, holding her tight.

She still doesn't understand why her mom's house? What was the crime? And did she ever do something to her mom? She didn't know how she found the trap door, only she knew about that.

Well, her and her dad.

The group held their
flashlights up, illuminating
its hideous features.

23. the scarecrow

Like most small towns, there's always some sort of phenomenon that occurs that can't be explained.

For Glenndale, out of the many, it would be the random appearance of the scarecrow.

It can be found in the field of Farmer Ben's farm, naturally, it's a cornfield. The crows would eat away at his corn, so he needed a solution and fast.

He couldn't allow those overgrown bats with feathers to take away the one advantage he had over the other farmers. He put in a request to the local newspaper if anyone could make the scariest scarecrow.

About a week later, a scarecrow was in his field. It was hard to ignore, and he first noticed it on his early morning walk.

It was tall, maybe ten feet. Its legs were out in a star formation, straws and sticks poking out of the arms and legs. Its face would make anyone think of a rotting pumpkin that's been stapled together.

It was gruesome.

The eyes were carved out and black marbles took their place. A smile slit apart from ear to ear and a gangly homemade straw hat.

The scarecrow startled Farmer Ben. Or rather, it scared him that this ugly being was suddenly in his field, but it seemed to work and he was no art critic so he kept it.

He asked around town who made the scarecrow, but no one came forward. Some came to see what the farmer was talking about and were astonished by the thing before them.

It brought so much attention and coverage, that the local newspaper interviewed Ben. Though it was good for his business, he said, he admitted that he had no idea who the creator was.

This made the newspaper like it even more. They raised the price of reward for anyone who would come forward as the artist. However, the scarecrow remained unclaimed in the farmer's field.

Parents called it hideous, it terrified kids, but teenagers saw this creature as a challenge.

At night, teens would get drunk and throw cans at it until Ben came out to scare them off.

It was especially a popular spot on Halloween. The story that would stick with the abomination was one of Vivian White.

* * *

Vivian and her classmates gathered around the scarecrow. The group held their flashlights up, illuminating its hideous features.

"They say that no one can find the artist because the creation before us killed him."

Everyone gathered close around her. Friends huddled up under the blanket they'd share, holding onto each other's hands.

"The creator saw the ad in the papers and wished to show the world the power of his art. He was a disgraced art student on account of his hideous artwork that would scare the professors. They called him unstable and unfit to be on their campus and expelled him. He needed to prove them wrong, so he sought out to make his last and greatest creation. That would surely gain the attention he had deserved all this time. It took him days non-stop to make this creation, but at the end of the week, his work was complete.

The scarecrow was made of sticks, hay, and mashed-up insects of the earth. The creator used some of his own blood to pump into the monster. But he had one more detail, the hat."

She pointed up to the unfinished and rushed hat. The scarecrow seemed to move against the wind in response.

"He would wait 'til morning to finish the hat, but he noticed out of the corner of his eyes the movement under the sheets. His creation. He moved the sheets to see the creature rise slowly, sitting up. Even sitting, he was the tallest piece the artist had ever made. The creator asked the creature a few yes or no questions.

'You can understand me?' And it nodded yes.

'Are you alive?' To which the scarecrow nodded yes.

'Do you know who I am?" Again a nod.

'Do you know who you are?' This time the scarecrow shook its head no.

"The creator was ecstatic. This creation, this blessed creation will make him rich and will make them pay. 'You are no longer some arts and craft project for a farmer, my creation you are art.' He said to the beast.

The creature wanted to disagree. It knew its purpose was to be something else, but it didn't wish to displease its master.

The man made a call outside, and he wished to sell the creation and put him up in the city. The creature was enraged. A feeling it's never felt before. The beast's very first feeling. It was enraged that its own creator, its own father, would give him away. So it attacked. In just one blow, the artist was dead.

The scarecrow, horrified by what it had done, wandered the night. It wandered until it stumbled into this very cornfield. To the very center, where it met the pole for it to be placed on. It climbed up and rested. For if anyone were to remove it from its spot, it would kill you and add your blood to the collection."

She finished and with that pause, the scarecrow began to shake.

A few people screamed and ran off, all tripping over one another. Vivian laughed and laughed as a few guys who were up on the scarecrow's post jumped down. They all gathered the remaining flashlights and walked off.

Though her story was fake, there were rumors of people checking out an artist who makes grotesque sculptures.

He lived on the outskirts of town. His house was empty and so was his shed where he worked. Though, on his desk was a design for a new straw hat.

THE DOPPELGÄNGER

'I must be you. I must take over,' the figure said with a voice just like his, 'there can only be one of us.'

24. the doppelgänger

"This has to be your laziest scary story ever, Viv," Morgan says, lying on the floor.

A bowl of popcorn between her and one of the twins. It was close to midnight as they all hung out in Morgan's basement after her babysitting gig.

"What? Listen here Cinderella. Doppelgängers are one of the most psychological tales that can make you sleep with one eye open." She says, pointing her beard down at Morgan.

The guy next to her leans his head back with a smile, his arm around her. He's dressed as Hades from *Hercules,* with his hair spiked and blue.

"Chill out dude, it's just one bad story. It's not like it's your whole career," he says.

The group ooh and ahh at his remark. Vivian pokes his side, but he holds her tighter.

"Who would've thought? The bully and the psychopath joining forces," one of the twins says, "may God have mercy on our souls." He says, grabbing a handful of m&ms.

"I think they're cute." The girl who traded her contacts back for her glasses says. She's leaning against a guy who's dressed as the Genie.

"Ugh, blah. Stop that Tanisha. You two are cute, not us. We're an experiment gone wrong," she says, but leans more into the boy dressed as Hades, "anyways silence, let me finish my story." She says, shushing everyone.

"He felt someone was watching him, following behind. Every turn he took, they took, and with every turn, they were close by. Slowly gaining on him. He decided to take a shortcut through the woods."

"First mistake," one of the twins cuts her off.

"Nah, the first mistake was letting them know where he lives," the boy dressed as the genie says.

"Guys. Shut up," Vivian groans, "so he took a shortcut through the woods. Until he reached a bridge, running across it he turned around. The figure appeared suddenly on the other side. It was terrifying how much they looked like him."

'What else do you want from me? What more can you take?' he asked, trying to stop his voice from wavering."

The figure didn't answer.

'You took my girlfriend away from me, all of my friends, and now my mother' he said, walking forward, 'Why am I being punished, why me?' He asked, stopping in the middle."

'I must be you. I must take over,' the figure said with a voice just like his, 'there can only be one of us.'

It stepped forward, as he stepped back. The figure pulled out a knife and ran towards him.

The man tripped as the figure lunged for him. They struggled until one was dead. And the other walked on."

She leans back for dramatic effect.

"The end?"

Morgan throws popcorn at her.

"I hate when you end stories like that."

"Don't hate the player, hate the game," she says, shrugging her shoulders.

"Boo!" The other twin says next to the girl dressed as Violet from *Charlie and the Chocolate Factory.*

They all laugh and scream "boo" while Vivian rolls her eyes.

* * *

Shortly after they all decide to head home. Vivian and the boy walk home together. They stop in front of her house now as he leans in to kiss her.

"That story was kinda scary and I don't think I can sleep alone now. Mind if I join you tonight?" He asks as they pull apart.

"You wish," she says, pushing him back with a smile.

She waves him off and heads inside, throwing her beard on the couch and plops down next to it. Her dog comes trotting in and hops up to sit on her lap.

She hears footsteps come down the stairs and her mom rounds the corner. Her mom lets out a scream enough to shake the house.

"Mom. What are you screaming for?" She asks, covering her ears.

"What are you doing?" She clutches her chest.

"Watching Tv, is that a crime?" She asks, crossing her arms.

"You said you'd be home by 11:30," she says, still sounding horrified.

"I texted you that I was gonna be a little late, you didn't answer."

"Honey, I just walked past your room, said goodnight, and you called back."

"Well that's impossible mom," she says, getting up now.

"I understand that," she hesitates, then looks at her, "if this is some kind of prank Vivian White. I promise you will not hear the end of it."

"I'm not a thirteen-year-old boy, mom. I don't prank," she says, going to the hall closet for a bat.

Then heading up the stairs, turning on all the lights as they go up. She heads to her room, her mom in tow, and slowly turns the knob and pushes the door open. She swings the bat around for a second, connecting with nothing. No one. She heads over to the lump on her bed and throws back the covers.

The dog they were babysitting curls up under her covers. He's pressing down on one of her old dolls that says "good night" with each squeeze of the stomach. The button must be worn out because it sounds lower. Similar to her voice. She picks up the doll and shows it to her mom.

"Oh, well. Solves that," she says, still looking terrified before walking off.

Vivian rolls her eyes but checks the rest of the room. Locking windows, checking her closet, before tossing the doll back in its bin.

"Alright, scoot over," she says, lying next to the dog. She keeps her lights on for right now.

The doll and the dog part makes sense, she thinks staring hard at her closet. But, she's kept that doll in the closet and hasn't taken it out in years.

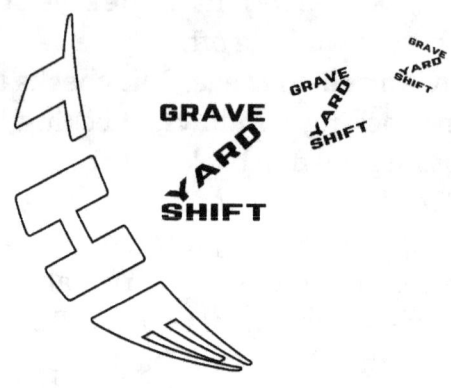

Working the graveyard shift
can start to do things
with your head.

25. the graveyard shift

Working at a sandwich shop has its perks. You get free sandwiches for lunch, the owner is a chill dude, and once in a while a pretty girl will come in and make your shift less miserable.

Well for the Hard Worker, he has so many jobs that the only available shift for weekdays is the graveyard shift. Which is arguably the best and worst shift ever.

It can be the best because no one comes in and it gives you a chance to get school work done.

The worst part is that the later it gets the crazier the people who come in are. No one is harmful, but weird. The Hard Worker usually works at the shop with another guy and they've seen some characters.

One time, there was a woman with one shoe and zombie makeup on despite it being weeks before Halloween. All she ordered was a cookie and some chips. She sat in the corner, stared at the wall for five minutes, then threw the cookies and chips away before leaving.

These people weren't any trouble, for the most part, and only on the occasion did they have to escort a few people out. The shift goes faster when someone is there to keep you company.

That wasn't gonna be the case tonight.

Tonight was gonna be especially rough for the Hard Worker. He finished his classes for that day and got   in five hours of working the front desk at the gym. It was about 7 pm and he just got a call from the other guy he works with at night. He tells him he has to stay home cause his son is sick. The Hard Worker didn't mind too much. It would give him time to take a break, but man will it be hard to stay awake. Thank goodness it's a Friday, so he could crash when he got home.

He gets in, cleans up, checks inventory, then sits down behind the counter begging with his eyes for no one to come in. All seems well for about two hours, but then he hears the door jingle open, and someone steps in. He gets up and walks over towards the counter.

"Hi, welcome to the Havana Sandwich Shop, how can I help you today?" He tries to sound less exhausted but falls flat.

"Hi," the guy says.

He's tall, definitely more than six feet, with a heavy black coat and top hat to match.

"You don't look too good there chap, perhaps you should lie down," he suggests with a hard cockney accent.

"I wish, but I'm on the clock." He rubs his eyes. Then he squints to get a better look at this guy, "wow, cool monocle, dude. Where'd you get it from?"

The tall gentleman seems to falter with the

question.

"Um, well. It actually belonged to this old man I used to take care of," he says, rubbing his hands.

"Cool, so you must have inherited it from him?"

"Something like that," he says, looking around.

"Cool, well would you like a sandwich, good sir?" He says in a botched accent.

Working the graveyard shift can start to do things with your head. Everything at this hour, especially after a long day, can make you laugh at nothing and act silly for no reason. It's your brain trying to shut down and sleep, but your body needs to keep going. The tall man looks at him then towards the menu.

"Um, I'll have a Cuban with extra mustard and olives, please," he says finally.

"Coming right up," He salutes, before making the sandwich.

He pulls out a knife to slice open the bread.

The flashing of the sharp object seems to remind the tall gentleman why he came in the first place. He reaches for the knife behind his back as the Hard Worker turns around to press the sandwich. The man leans a little over the counter, his arms are long enough.

"You know, no one has ever asked for olives on their Cuban or on a sandwich in general. Bold choice my man." The Hard Worker says, his back still turned.

The guy stops his motion and retracts his knife.

"Really? Everyone hates olives?"

"Not me dude. I like 'em, very underrated food. Plus, olives are the least weird thing you can order," he says, turning back as the guy quickly hides his knife.

"Really? Like what?" The man asks.

"Well, one guy asked for anchovies with his sandwich and just that, but we all have taste, ya know, so who am I to judge?"

The Hard Worker also gets oddly wise at this hour and the tall man was along for the ride it seems. They talk as the gentleman eats his sandwich. Leaving behind a tip, the man walks out and the Hard Worker clocked out a few hours later.

* * *

The next morning, the hard worker crashed on his couch, wakes up to a phone call.

"Hey man, what's up?" He says to his boss.

"John, I was looking over the cameras from last night. Who were you talking to?"

"Some dude," he says groovily, then sits up, "Oh crap, did he forget to pay. Did I let him walk out with a sandwich for free?"

"No, and if that were the case it doesn't matter. Have you seen this dude before?"

"No, why?"

"He's a criminal, John. A serial killer. He's the gentleman killer," he says softly.

"A criminal," John says distantly.

"John, I don't know what you did, but whatever it was it kept you alive. He could've and would've killed you, what did you do? Are you good?" He says, "John. John!"

"I thought maybe he was a dream. He was so, so tall," John says quietly, dropping the phone as his boss continues to call his name.

LAKE SHORE DRIVE

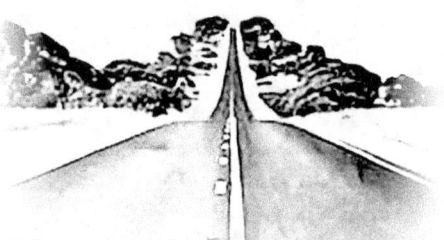

They all decided, some by
choice, to stay out after the
sun went down.

26. lake shore drive

There's a lake right on the border of town. As the summer starts, every teen in town heads to the lake for a swim.

Like clockwork spends the first weeks of summer on the lake. It's usually early afternoon leading into the night. Once again, every teen knows better than to stay out after the sun goes down.

It's that summer for these teens. Their last summer together before they all go off to college. For some a relief and for others a painful time. They all decided, some by choice, to stay out after the sun went down. They have the whole lake to themselves.

Why had no one thought of it before?

* * *

"Why has no one thought of it before?" One of the guys says, throwing another stick into the fire.

"Probably 'cause the people dumb like us were never heard from again." One of the girls says, pulling her sweater tight around her.

"Aww come on Abby," he pulls her close to his side, "I'll protect you."

She smiles up at him and snuggles closer into him. Making sure that he can feel her press into him.

"Yea, Ms. White. What happened to that energy when you were doing a flip off the tire swing earlier?" A louder girl says.

Her bathing suit is still exposed, still dripping in her lawn chair. Abby rolls her eyes at her. She's always annoyed at Ann Marie without her having to do a single thing.

"It was bright and early then, but now I'm very aware that it's just us in these woods." She says, pushing off of the guy to sit up higher.

"I agree with Abby. God knows what's out here," a small, quiet girl says, still wrapped in her towel.

"Thank you, Penny," Abby says.

"Aww come on guys," a voice says, crashing through the bushes.

Another guy in tow with her, "This is our last summer together," she says, walking to the center. She looks at all of them.

"We're all going away. Penny's off to Oklahoma. Francine, you're going backpacking in Columbia. Abby you're going to the college just down the road rooming with Tory," she laughs.

"Ugh, don't remind me," Abby rolls her eyes.

"Ann, you and Dominic are off to the Air Force, and Perry's off to UCLA," she says, looking down.

She rubs her sneakers on the ground. Perry comes up behind her and takes her in his arms.

"And you're off to New York," he looks at the group, "what she's trying to say is that this might be the last time we see each other for a while. We might as well do something stupid at least once in a while," he finishes.

They all nod, roused by their speeches. The girl looks up at her boyfriend.

"Something stupid like what Perry?" She smiles.

"Aww come on Jo, use that imagination of yours," he says, tickling her sides.

He laughs as she pushes him away. The group looks at them.

Perfect.

They're the perfect couple and the glue that holds their group together. They don't have the energy to tell them that they are the only reason they're all still friends and will remain friends until they all leave. So they'll pretend just for tonight.

"Alright, enough of this. I'm taking a dip. A skinny dip," Ann Marie says, wiggling her eyebrows.

Dominic looks up at her, his eyebrows raised in question, and then she's running off toward the docks.

"Hell yeah," Joann says, running off after her.

Francine gets up too.

"Come on Penny," she says.

"No, I'll watch y'all, but I'm not going in nude."

"Why not Pen? It'll be fun," Dominic says.

He stands up and strips his shorts, running off. Later on, they hear screams and many splashes.

Penny reluctantly walks to the deck and sits down. Perry sits down next to her.

"Don't touch my girlfriend, man," he calls out for his friend.

They all laugh. Abby hops in last, making her way over to Dominic.

The water isn't too deep. Maybe five feet closer to the dock. They all hover around one another. No one goes further than twenty feet. Perry watches Joann tread water for a bit. She smiles up at him. He smiles back. Then she turns around and screams.

"Something brushed my leg."

Perry leans forward, not jumping in yet.

"Gurl, it's probably seaweed," Ann Marie says, splashing Francine.

They all go back to their business for a bit, but then Joann screams again.

This time going down.

"Jo!" Perry shouts, jumping into the water.

He wades over. The others scream as Perry looks around for Joann. They hear a splash towards the center of the lake, which is about forty feet away from the docks. And then a gasp for air.

"Perry!" She screams.

He rushes over and scoops her into his arms. She clings to him, wrapping her arms around his neck.

"It's okay, it's okay," he says, stroking her hair and pulling her closer.

"I felt like I was being pulled down further and further. It felt like I kept sinking and sinking." She coughs out, shaking against him.

He holds her all the way back, but he looks around some more for any other signs of life or air bubbles. The strangest part was that the lake isn't that deep; the water was only six feet deep in the center.

The Coach was the best there was, he was goofy, annoyingly optimistic, and one helluva soccer player.

27. the coach

If there's one sport that Glenndale would leave town for, it has to be soccer; well, it's their kid's soccer team anyways.

The Glenndale Ducks are the name and kicking butt is their game. They were pretty good too, not FIFA good, but good enough to make it to championships every single year. They had the heart and the dedication to remain a team ever since they were five.

They were still doing good when a few of their members disappeared in the woods about ten years ago. When the kids came back, everyone from the original team was able to come back to Glenndale; greeting one another as if they hadn't mourned them.

Even the Coach for the original team was able to see all the kids one last time before he passed away.

The Coach was the best there was, he was goofy, annoyingly optimistic, and one helluva soccer player. All of the members, grown and "young" came together for his funeral and went out for drinks afterward.

* * *

"What are we gonna do now?" Romona asks, nursing her beer.

She was technically the oldest of the group, but with the body of a thirteen-year-old, you wouldn't have guessed it.

"What do you mean?" Joseph looks at her. He was twenty-three now and was her best friend.

"I mean, our parents want us to get back to our normal lives. It's like they want to carry on as if it didn't happen. As if I'm not a twenty-three-year-old in a kid's body." She rocks the bottle back and forth.

The other "kids" around her nod.

"It's true. They want to protect us, so out of all of the things they can control. You know, taking us to school and practice." The blonde kid, David, says.

"Practice," Gina says, technically the youngest of the group at age twenty-two, "won't be the same without Coach."

They all nod in unison, drinking in silence for a bit.

"You know, when he heard you guys went missing, he made us pray every game we played. Even the new teammates took a silent prayer," Joseph says quietly.

"He didn't know how to start, so our devoted Christian had to help him. He kept cutting off Lucy," Regina says with a smile.

"It was ridiculous. He kept repeating everything I said." Lucy agrees, covering her mouth to hide her smile.

They all laugh and smile at the memory of him.

"My mom told me who the new coach was. It's some guy named Harold," David says, turning to Pat, his best friend since they were babies.

"Harold sounds like an accountant," Pat says, kicking Lucy's knee.

"Oh stop, we all aren't that bad, but I am sure he'll be just as boring and blah as his name."

They all howl with laughter, a few people around them turn in their direction.

To the average person, it looks as if five adults are giving six kids a drink. The townspeople know how close these kids are. They turn back around and give those kids some respect.

"Do y'all remember when Coach told us his name?" Romona asks, gripping her sides at the thought.

"Oh my gosh, yes," Paulo says, grabbing Romona's arm, "he made us swear to not laugh."

"He said. He said that his first name was Bernie," Regina struggles to get out, leaning against Peter, "and then he said his last name was Macdonald the sixth." She finishes and they all laugh, some choking on their drinks.

"Oh lord. I died on the sixth part. He told us that if he ever had kids he'd never give them the name Bernie," Lucy says, wiping her eyes.

"Well, I would hope not. What a terrible name to last that long," Gina says.

"Well here's to Bernie and his ridiculous name." David raises his bottle.

They all raise their drinks, feeling a little bit better.

* * *

It's getting late and the "kids" have a big first day of soccer practice tomorrow, so they all walk home together.

"Don't let mommy know that you were out drinking," Pat slurs to David.

"Hey. You let your beautiful mom know that I'll see her later tonight," David shouts back.

They all laugh and run away from each other before getting back home. The most normal they've probably felt in a long time.

The next morning, all the parents drive their kids to practice where they meet their new teammates and Harold.

"He's exactly like I pictured. Look at his mustache," Paulo whispers to Del.

They both chuckle and push each other away.

"Alright kiddos, huddle up, don't be shy," Harold says with a sort of Minnesota accent, "now I'm gonna be your new coach. My name is Harold Goldenfeld," the kid's try not to look at each other or they'll start laughing again, "but you can call me Coach Goldenfeld."

"Uh sir," Paulo raises his hand.

The gang hits him to shut up, but Goldenfeld takes the bait.

"Uh yes sir, what can I do for ya?"

"How about we call you Coach Goldfinger? You look like you were an amazing Goalie," Paulo says innocently.

The gang all cough loud into their arms to cover their laughs.

"Allergies," they all say.

"Hmm, I like that name. Though I was a striker, I like the name kid." Coach Goldfinger says.

They all chuckle and push each other as he rattles on. They can practically hear Coach telling them to stop being wise-asses.

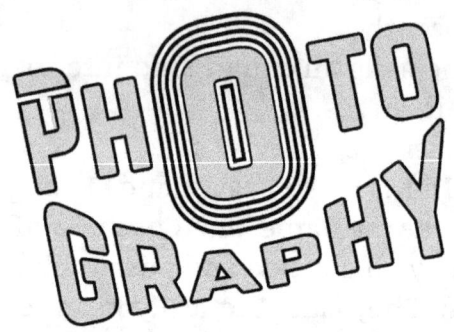

A few days later, she's in the
woods looking for
her picture.

28. photography

"You have a good eye, Romona." Her teacher says.

"Thanks," she says quietly.

Out of all her friends, she was the only one who was into photography. There isn't an official Glenndale photography club, except for the one in high school and the exception of a small class in middle school.

Even after her return, it was the one thing that kept her calm.She looks around at the other kids in her group. They were all sitting in one of the art classrooms at the middle school.

She didn't have to go to school or attend any of the classes, but her mother encouraged her to at least keep up photography.

"Class, though her camera isn't as advanced as the rest of y'all, she still was able to catch a bird in motion and the nest. Where was this taken?"

"The nook of our shed. There's a little overhanging part that protects them from the rain."

"And what did it mean to you?" She asks, as the class swivels their heads to Romona.

"Uh, I don't know. I just thought it was beautiful...," she trails off, avoiding the eyes.

"Hmm, interesting," she gives a look before turning towards the class, "okay kids. Following this weekend, I want y'all to take a picture of something that has impacted your life, good or bad. Give me some depth." She flashes a smile.

Romona walks out of the class, her mom waiting on the curb to pick her up.

"How was class, honey?"

"Good. She liked the bird picture."

"Well, that's nice."

Her mom looks as if she wants to say more, Romona just sits and waits as they drive off.

"Honey, our birdie had three baby birds, but one of them didn't make it. It fell." She says, looking forward.

Romona just stares straight ahead too.

It fell, she thinks as she grips the seatbelt a little tighter.

✳ ✳ ✳

A few days later she's in the woods looking for her picture. The one thing that changed her life.

She's nervous. Has been every time she even drives by it. She's tried so hard to go back and at least sit comfortably in there as she did before, but she gets emotional each time.

Now she's only twenty feet in and she already feels sick to her stomach, but she needs to do this. She can't live in fear anymore, so she walks slowly through the woods. Leaves crunching underneath her. She slowly crests a small hill and there it was.

* * *

"Alright, good job Barry. I love the meaning behind you holding your mother's hand, very beautiful," she looks around, "alright now. Romona, what have you got for us today?"

Romona stands up and displays her photo on the projector.

"Oh, I see, um," her teacher lost at words, "Romona honey, please explain your photo."

"It's a Pileated Woodpecker."

"I see, yes well. I asked you to take a picture of something that has affected you."

"I know, and that's what I did."

"No, it's not Romona," she takes off her glasses to rub the bridge of her nose, "What about the arch? The one thing that affected your life greatly?" She says with frustration.

Romona turns to face her.

"I had a life before the arch you know," she says calmly, "I was impacted before the arch. You wouldn't think that, but my life wasn't defined by one of the moments in my life. You asked for anything that's impacted us. Birds. I used to be part of a birdwatching group. We would listen to bird calls, identifying them, and I'd always bring a camera around and take pictures. I love taking pictures of them because my group has been with me since I was a kid. It made me like taking pictures."

The teacher looks ashamed now, turning her head down in a bow as the students look around confused.

"I haven't been in those woods since I came back. The fact that I went yesterday to take a few pictures of something that makes me happy should be enough. I'm tired of this pretentious B.S. with pictures. A picture doesn't have to mean everything all the time. Our impacts are our own," she says. Taking her picture and leaving.

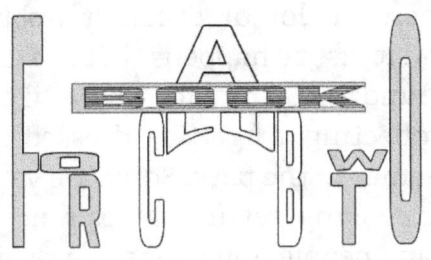

There's a lot of different
hobbies in the world, and it
just so happens that the
strange ones can be found
in Glenndale.

29. a book club for two

There's a lot of different hobbies in the world, and it just so happens that the strange ones can be found in Glenndale. Some like whittling, marble collecting, or getting dressed up for role-playing games in the park. Some are very mild and tame, like cooking, sewing, or reading.

Many people don't consider reading to be a hobby, but much like any other hobby, you can pick up reading at any time. There are loads of book clubs in Glenndale. Most end up talking about anything but the book, but the people in it usually come together again each time for more than the book.

❊ ❊ ❊

"Hey, you got different frames," Alex says, greeting her in their corner.

"Uh, yea. You know the others weren't doing it for me," Tanisha says, sitting down.

It's the following Monday after Halloween, and Tanisha and Alex are meeting for their book club. After a little convincing, she decided to join him.

"So I'm guessing you didn't get much

reading done?" She asks.

"How could you tell?" He smiles, trading seats to sit next to her.

"Well for starters you look like you haven't slept at all, and the bookmark tells all." She points.

They both look at his bookmark in a spot very close to the beginning.

"Yea, my older sister's birthday was yesterday and I didn't really sleep 'til three, and school kicked my butt today."

"Yea, physics will be the death of me." She nods.

"College level?"

"Regular Physics is enough for me," she says.

He laughs and she laughs too. He stops to smile at her.

"Uh, so I read on and we find out. Spoiler, Anthony's right, his mother isn't dead. She did leave and he's trying to find out what she's up to." Tanisha dives right in, trying hard not to notice his gaze on her.

"Mhmm," Alex says.

She can't ignore how he's getting closer to her.

"Uh, so I was wondering what you thought of Anthony so far?" She asks as her voice wavers, but not moving an inch.

If he continues his path he is sure to kiss her, and on instinct, she moves back. He notices and stops.

"Oh, I'm sorry. I thought that on Halloween," he says, leaning back, "I thought. I'm sorry. I should go," he starts to pack up.

"No wait," she says, "please stay and let me explain myself."

He sits back down, careful not to touch her.

"I like books. I've loved reading them ever since I was young. It was my time to escape the reality of my crazy life and imagine myself in a different crazy world," she pauses, "and it sounds like a lame hobby to have. There are so many cool hobbies to do, but I like reading 'cause I can relate to those kids in the books."

She scoots her legs under her and leans into her words more.

"I like Anthony cause he's more than an asshole, he has a reason. He's hurt, broken, beaten down over and over again, but he knows what he knows. He doesn't let anyone tell him anything different anymore. He's tough despite being beaten down a couple of times."

She looks up at him finally.

"You didn't mistake anything on Halloween. I've had a crush on you ever since we were kids. I guess I've always imagined the moment, but I always think I'm not good enough for people. Maybe I'm wrong to believe that I can have anything good. But characters like Anthony inspire me to keep getting up and know that I'm worth it." She says, putting her hand between them.

He reaches down to rest his on hers.

"So, you've always had a crush on me?"

"Oh I knew this would go to your head," she says, trying to scoot away, but he leans forward again.

"No, let's discuss that." He teases.

"No. Back to the book, you have to catch up," she says, laughing, and pushing him away.

They hardly opened up the book that day, but the Crush and the Granddaughter found a better hobby. A hobby can do that to people, winning them over constantly without doing a thing.

HOSPITAL
DAZE

The hospital is busier than usual.

30. hospital daze

The ones that go to the hospital in Glenndale are usually in for stupid reasons. Though some doctors tell the patient that they aren't stupid for getting into the situation, it's a lie.

The hospital is always busy, and especially around the holidays. Strangely enough, even around the holidays you least suspect. One of Dr. Oak's crazy patient stories consists of a man who was dared to light a small bonfire using propane on Flag day. Long story short it was not a small bonfire, he had third-degree burns, and part of his pants melted onto his skin.

Most cases involving these types of injuries are either dares or not reading the instructions. One guy, for example, gorilla glued a toupee to his head but found out during a date that he was allergic to the glue.

However, there are times where serious injuries and victims of accidents come to the hospital.

The mayor and the young lady who also lost her life at the scene of the car crash were wheeled in on a day like any other. It was all hands on deck to save both lives. The girl was in bad shape, but her family still wanted them to try and revive her if they could. They picked up a heartbeat, but she hemorrhaged and later passed away.

The mayor, however, had a punctured lung and was struggling to breathe. Many people were moving around his body, but they were able to keep him out of critical condition with enough time for his wife to visit.

She wasn't the pristine or organized mayor's wife they were all so used to seeing. She was crying, clinging, and gripping her husband's hand. He pulled her close and whispered something in her ear. She backed away and wouldn't stop shaking her head and his hand. He faded away, and to watch his wife go into shock was one of the saddest cases that Dr. Oak had ever seen.

It's being a doctor that most people fear. To be responsible for a life, as if to play God, but you have no instructions. Just facts and hopes that everything else will turn out alright. Dr. Oak has lost people on the job, and it's hard to tell family and friends that their loved one has passed. He tries to keep his mind on the two things that push him to be where he is now. The drive of hope is one of them.

It's the world's most powerful drug, and once lost it's hard to get back. The second thing that fuels his drive to keep going on is his daughter. He loves her more than his very own life. He doesn't say it as often as he should and no matter how messed up his life is there's no excuse for not telling her.

He decided that after his shift was over he'd treat her. Surely the hospital could function a few hours without him. He picks up takeout and flowers for her, and as he sets the food on the table and gets a vase for the flowers he calls out to her. No answer.

Even on his least busy days, she texts or calls him to let him know if she's at a friend's house or practice. He calls out to her one last time before climbing the stairs towards her room. The lights are on, so she's probably not asleep. He pushes the door open, and there she was lying on a towel. Her face was pale and her hair matted. In her hand was a letter opener with blood streaming down her arms.

* * *

The hospital is busier than usual. It's Labor Day weekend. There are pool accidents and firework mishaps, but no one is in critical condition. Dr. Oak comes barreling through the door yelling at his staff to help. His daughter drooping in his arms like a wilted flower, the blood caking them both. His top nurse and best friend Mandy comes first with the gurney and they carry Jackie off down the hall. Dr. Oak hot on their tails.

"She's blood type O, no allergies or past medical emergencies." Dr. Oak says, his voice wavering.

It throws everyone off, as his staff has never seen him like this, out of scrubs and looking like a nervous wreck.

"We have her blood type on sight," Mandy says softly.

"Me. Take my blood, please," Dr. Oak says desperately.

Some patients throughout the hall look as he runs along with his daughter's gurney.

"Daddy's coming Jackie. He's coming and he loves you," he says, grabbing her hand. He doesn't let go for a second, not even to wipe the tears.

STARGAZING

Nothing more than you,
your partner, the stars, and
every other person who can't
take a hint.

31. star gazing

"The point of stargazing is to watch the stars," she says next to him.

"I understand," he says.

"But...?"

"But why stare at the stars when I can stare at something more beautiful?" He smiles as she blushes a little.

Stargazing is less of a hobby or even a fun activity to do with friends, but more like the world's greatest pickup line. Every couple of course wants to pick up at least one activity they can do together. It gives them, if not one, another thing they have in common. Even hanging out at the farmer's market every weekend is an activity in itself. Stargazing just so happens to be one of the most romantic ones. Nothing more than you, your partner, the stars, and every other person who can't take a hint.

"How come you never talk to me like that anymore Harold?" A wife complains to her husband in the next car over.

"Honey, not right now," Harold says, breathing out a sigh.

The thing about these activities, like stargazing, is that it's more of a town thing than an individual thing. There's only one good spot to watch the stars late at night, so why not join everyone else to watch them.

"You know when I had this place in mind to watch the stars with you, I thought maybe we'd be alone," Ian whispers.

"Well, that's the thing about this town, it's so small that we're all on top of each other. It's hard to be in one place alone." Ellie laughs.

"So it seems, maybe we should go?"

"No, I'm having a good time," she says, squeezing his arm, "Lemme at least point out a couple of constellations."

"Yeah, we won't be too much trouble. Won't we Missy?" Harold says to his wife.

"How dare you—" she starts as Harold rolls up the window.

The couple isn't wrong though. Usually, when you want to do one thing by yourself or with your partner, it's most likely a class with other people. It's hard to be a photographer or someone who does embroidery without five people wanting to join you. However, some people would rather be left on their own. Take the Bodyguard for example as he tries to ignore Missy and Harold arguing.

"Okay, so that's the Little Dipper, right next to it is the Big Dipper. And you see that red tiny dot right there," she says, leaning into him, "that's Mars."

"Wow, you know a lot about space," he says, leaning back into her.

She covers her smile with her hands.

"You know. I didn't grow up in this town. I came here about ten years ago, but growing up my parents didn't have time for me. I had a sister, but she was way older than me and I didn't have a whole lot of friends, but books were my friends. And the stars were my friends too," she says, looking back up, "I learned all about the constellations, the planets, the moon, and everything about space. It was one of the many things I did on my own. Then I moved here and it's like everyone is part of this really big family. Maybe I love this town so much 'cause whatever happens we do it as a family, and I never really had that."

She smiles up at him, then turns to face the stars again as she leans into him. They're silent and all is dark except for the stars above.

Then he finished the last
detail: her wooden eyes.

32. woodcarving

There is only one cabin in the woods, but no one besides the woodcarver is there. He used to teach a woodshop class out in the woods.

He's tough and burly, almost seven feet tall. It would take him about two swings just to knock down one tree. He'd carry it back for the class and divide it into sections for each group. Some would carve small furniture, others made clothespins and animal carvings. He'd have a station just for whittling and show the class how to properly shape the wood into how you wanted it to look. He'd always make a wooden person as an example. His wife would walk by and tell them each time that that was supposed to be her. They'd all laugh with her and he'd smile each time.

That was years ago, and the woodcarver lives alone now. He canceled all his classes. People understood his reasoning, but later just moved on to a different task. They get to move on, but he can't. At first, he whittled all of the adults and all the kids who took his class.

There was one lady who would come in making all of these gifts for her son and father. She showed him the pictures and explained what she hopes to make that day. The woodcarver would give her a kind smile, soft eyes, and an older man in one hand and a young boy in the other.

There was a girl about fourteen years old who was born blind. She would come in with her mom, but she wouldn't need her most of the time. She would feel the wood as if understanding it, getting to know it again like an old friend. She was strong for her age. Her mom said she was a swimmer, so he gave her muscles holding a tree, trying to wrap her arms all the way around.

He used to just make his students, but ever since five years after that, all he's been carving is his wife. The sizes would range from as small as his palm to five feet tall. Each would show her as she was. She was graceful like the leaves in the breeze, sturdy like a tree trunk, but nurturing and spreading love like roots. His workshop was a reminder of her, a museum, a dedication, and his love. His workshop had become his pain.

He's out now, it's pouring hard enough for him to be soaked to the bone, but he can see well enough. He brought his ax up and sliced it into the tree. He hits hard, but was careful with where he hit. He cut out the frame, then he brought finer tools out to whittle away. He closes his eyes now and lets the rain wash over him like a dream. He knew every curve, done it a thousand times, and every detail he was sure of. Then he finished the last detail: her wooden eyes.

Opening his own, he stared into them. A carving of about her size stared up at him, cupping his face with a sort of sadness behind them. He reached out to hold her wooden hands, as he feels a pair of eyes on his back.

"I understand that these are your woods. I'm sorry on that part," he says to the eyes behind him, "but she was my wife, and I can't move on," he chokes up.

"How can I? She was my everything and now I can't get her eyes out of my head. I can't leave her, can't stop creating her, hoping she comes back, but I know she can't."

The figure says nothing, but he knows that someone is behind him just staring. The woodcarver stands up straight now, holding the carving one last time.

"I know. I know," he mumbles to himself.

He turns around, but his eyes land on no one. Just him and the rain.

"Goodbye, my love. Until we meet again." He walks off, the ax dragging behind him.

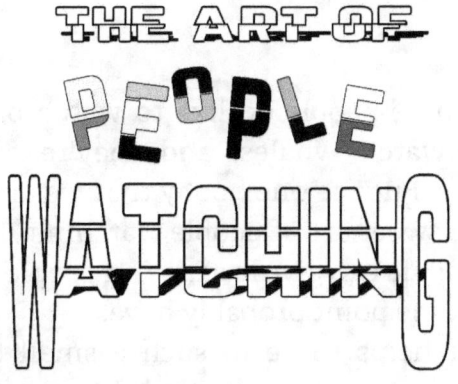

THE ART OF PEOPLE WATCHING

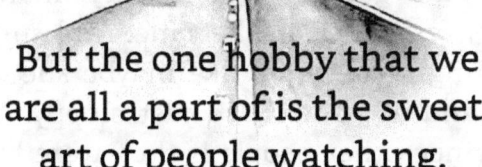

But the one hobby that we
are all a part of is the sweet
art of people watching.

33. the art of people watching

Some people do like to watch birds, some like to watch whales, and they're even cloud watchers. But the one hobby that we are all a part of is the sweet art of people watching. The people of Glenndale can give lectures on people watching, and at some point probably have.

It helps to be in such a small town that allows people to enhance their imagination. With a larger town, there is no way that everybody can make up convincing lives for the people that pass them. For those in smaller towns living on top of one another helps you create a double life.

Take the Librarian, for example, the study group that goes to the library makes up a double life for her all the time. And sure, saying something so extreme like maybe she's an alien is fun and all, but that's just sloppy. You need to convince other people if they were to ask you about the person, and they have to believe you.

The group picks up on the little facts to build a story. Every day she changes her hair bow, she's dedicated to being a librarian, she runs this place, but she has a secret that she thinks no one knows.

The Librarian and the Bodyguard, who the

kid's found out his name to be Ian, are seeing each other. They make her a target or anyone for that matter, and they "investigate". They aren't stalker-level invested, but the casual kind. If they spot her while out or in a public place they make a mental note and bring it back to the group at the end of the week. They were able to connect the pieces from each member. Tanisha saw her and the Bodyguard at the YMCA for an art class. Morgan saw them having dinner at a restaurant when she was out with her family. Vivian has seen them a bunch of times at the library.

They make predictions with all the information they have, like what their futures might hold based on the path they take.

A chunk of their people-watching projects takes place in the library. It's where people claim to have book clubs and study groups alike, but once the meetings are over they take an opportunity to snoop.

The study group likes to also spy on classmates. They see people from their physics class, some were ex-lovers and they think that one was a master manipulator based on the way they walk in together. They see Jackie O. chilling by herself and a boy who they all know has a girlfriend gawking at her. In a way, it's like they have the power to destroy and tear down the lives of these people with the dirt they've collected.

Well, except for the Bodyguard.

This guy is new territory, so the kids

decided to make him their next project. Some justifying him by saying to protect the Librarian, but they all know that they just want to find something on this guy. They never run into him in any other public place besides the library, and he's almost everywhere with the Librarian. The one time he wasn't, Tanisha pointed out, was at the grocery store.

"What did he get?" Vivian, the leader of the people watching club/study group says.

"Nothing out of the ordinary: cereal, eggs, oranges, a bag of dog food, and basic hygienic stuff. I ran a couple of scenarios, but no dice," she finishes.

"Hmm, this is tough. I've talked to him a couple of times before my mom's meetings, but ever since they stopped meeting about a week ago my trail has run dry."

They all understood that these were made-up scenarios and that of course, it's normal to have a few secrets. Who doesn't, but never has this club not been able to find something on anybody.

"We'll have to talk to Miss Ellie about him," Morgan says as they climb the stairs to the library.

"You think she'll just give up her new boyfriend like that?" Vivian asks, pulling the doors open, "we'll have to be sneaky and really not give ourselves away..." she trails off.

The library was a mess. People were lining up almost to the door to checkout with the world's oldest librarian manning the line. The people among the mess trying to serve themselves hot chocolate in the back. There were lots of books that needed to be reshelved, and children running around. The group pushes its way towards the front.

"Hey, what's going on?" Vivian shouts over the crowd.

"Ellie is gone. She didn't show up to work this morning," The older librarian shouts back.

MOTION

Did she capture them
perfectly?

34. stop motion

The town was down to a science. Everything in its place, every person in their place, and no stone unturned. Every tree, every building, every single detail from the cracks on the town hall building to the bumper sticker on a townsperson's car were correct. She didn't know all their names, but it didn't matter, because she knew how they would look.

Patty Johnson made a tiny replica of the town of Glenndale. It had gotten so big that there was hardly any room in her basement, so she moved to an abandoned warehouse. The conditions were good and the lighting was perfect, and as a bonus, no one has caught her yet.

It's not the Mailman who's the greatest people watcher and it's not even the study group. She is the all-seeing, all-powerful Oz of Glenndale. You could see her up in a police lineup and not know who she was. She was forgotten, left behind, in the background, but it's no matter to her. She likes it in the shadows.

She wasn't born here, but she has lived here long enough to consider herself a local. Nobody joined her but her little town. She started it years ago. Felt something telling her that she needed to start this. Call it a gut feeling. So, she started off making all the people. All 4,998. Well by then it would be 5,018, but no matter, she'd find out about them soon enough.

The Mayor's Wife, the Librarian, even the Coach who is soon to pass. She pictured their clothes, their hair that morning, their expressions. All of it she knew. She moved onto the kids, those alive and "dead". She got what they would wear and their relationships with one another. She had it all.

That's when she moved over to the warehouse to start constructing the town.

She must have been the favorite customer of the craft store because she would gather all the clay. By the next time they stocked up, she'd be back again. She ordered bundles of material and string to make the fine details on the buildings. She even added the warehouse in the middle of the woods to her display. There were two things she still needed. And today was the last time to get them done before it happened.

"Hello hello," she says to the cashier at the craft store.

"Hey Miss Patty," Janelle says.

She didn't have to restock the shelves, so she didn't care that Patty took all the supplies. She wanders the aisles, picking up things here and there, and filling up her cart to the top.

"Wow, I can't even stick to one hobby. I feel like you've been working on this long before I was working here."

"Oh, it's more than a hobby now, my dear. It has become a part of my life if you will, and yes. Almost five years in a couple of days."

"Dedication," she says, swiping all the products.

"Thank you, my dear. I should be done tonight."

She pays and Janelle helps her put all the bags in the cart.

"Well, good luck," she says, waving goodbye, "And don't forget to bring back that cart."

Walking back towards the woods. She gets a feeling in the air like the big thing is coming, so she makes a pit stop at the grocery store.

"Just this bottle of syrup?" John says, swiping the bottle.

"I'll be back for other things, but I just need this right now."

"Well you're in luck, that's our last bottle for a couple of days."

He checks out her bottle as she continues her journey back to the warehouse in the woods. They're huge and lush, surrounding the town like a noose rather than a blanket. Her warehouse is in the woods along with the arch and the man with the arrows.

She molds and adds a truck at the edge of the town, then thinks for a minute. She pulls out some of the clay, peeling the side of the truck like a banana. She grabs her bottle of syrup and squeezes it into the truck, laughing a little as she goes.

"Perfect," she says, finishing up. Knocking over a few tiny people into the syrupy mess.

She licks her fingers a little as she heads out, stopping once again for the groceries, and returning the shopping cart. She heads back to the house and reaches for the secret door just as a little girl stumbles out.

"Ahh yes, this is your house, not so little one." She says after they stare at each other for some time.

The cops greet her not too long after, pushing her to the ground as the girl's mother screams in horror.

"You all should check out my display in the woods. It's beautiful, simply beautiful," she says, cackling, "can't miss it, the big warehouse. I've been working on it for years," she says, getting hauled up and shoved into the police car.

She laughs the whole ride over, what they would think of her replica. Did she capture them perfectly?

...,but things went from
sweet to sour in the last
fifteen minutes of the ride.

35. first dates

If there was such a thing as a perfect first date, it would belong in a parallel universe.

First dates are weird. It's like choosing a partner for a class that you haven't worked with before. It gets awkward too soon and it ends up with one person trying too hard to keep up the conversation.

There are plenty of places to go for first dates, but whichever one picked will set the tone for the rest of the date.

There are a few mom-and-pop restaurants around town, but it's a shame that everyone's eaten at every place since birth. Kids who want to date or who are going on a first date have to be creative and still stay within the perimeters of the law.

Most kids when they start dating are around middle school age or in the ballpark of not owning a car. They can only stay within the town limits unless they dare to ask their parents for a ride. They try out picnics in the parks, apple picking, arcades, the old theater, and fireworks shows.

Most of these dates take place outside and as far as first dates go, they go pretty well. It gets a little more complicated when the kids reach high school. The actual effort has to be put into the dates now.

One of the most elaborate first dates in the history of all of Kenneth Wheeler High school was the hot air balloon ride incident.

It's been done before. In fact, plenty of proposals start that way, but this one was probably the most tragic and yet romantic one ever.

* * *

Stacey McIntosh and David Bowerman went out onto the open field reserved for the Fourth of July fireworks in 2015. That would give them three hours before the fireworks went off. They were prepped and strapped in with a picnic basket and blanket, and then the instructor and the couple went up at around 5:30pm.

They remained in the air and were expected to land in another field at around 6:45pm. That would place them about a safe hour before the fireworks would go off.

During that time, David poured Stacey a bottle of sparkling grape juice. They ate little sandwiches and exchanged soft smiles followed by quick glances.

The instructor admitted that day he felt like was part of the problem. Even a little embarrassed that he was unintentionally third-wheeling. The instructor also noted that the date so far was going really well from his perspective. Even he could've been fooled that these two have been dating a long time based off of the enormous amount of effort put into the date.

The sun was setting around the time they were nearing the end of their balloon trip. At about 6:30pm, the two stood up to look over the town. David looked at Stacey and she looked over at him. One might predict that at this point they would've kissed, but things went from sweet to sour in the last fifteen minutes of the ride.

Somehow, "Romeo" brought up politics and compared it to the sunset they were watching.

As a note to all young people, never bring up politics on the first date. Definitely don't try to find a way to compare it to the sunset too.

Stacey tensed up and softly countered what he said. David rebutted, not taking the hint, and Stacey countered. This argument went on for about five minutes to which the last ten minutes they segregated themselves as far as they could in a hot air balloon.

The instructor noted that he couldn't wait to reach the ground, probably more than these two.

They touched down at about 6:47pm and before the hot air balloon was fully on the ground, David hopped down and stormed off. One of the attendants who was helping bring the hot air balloon back yelled after him. He stopped once he saw the tears running down David's face. Stacey waited until the basket was on the ground and stomped after David. She cursed him out for not helping her out of the balloon.

After all that, at around 7:15pm the instructor and the attendant finished up the hot air balloon. They noticed that the couple had left behind their basket and looted it for leftovers.

They both sat in the field as the sun dipped low in the sky. The instructor confessed how awkward it got and how ambitious this boy was for the first date. The attendant asked what went wrong. The instructor told him that by this first date that their relationship would've been a disaster from the start.

They laughed, drank, and talked until the fireworks started. As far as first dates go, there are do's and don't. The two kid's disaster of a first date is an example of what never ever to do. Ever. Too big is scary, easing into dates and not bringing up politics is a must. The do's would be how for the first time that the instructor and the attendant hung out together. They became closer friends, exchanged numbers to hang out more, and watched the fireworks.

As far as the Fourth of July of 2015, there was a tragic date. Even though nothing happened to cause any damage, Stacey and David will never want to see each other again.

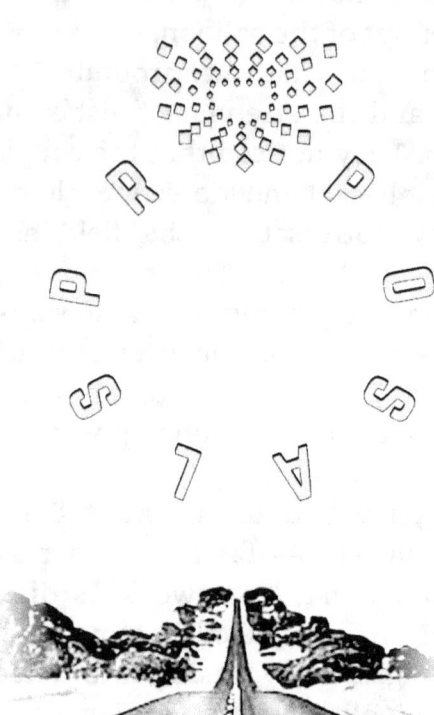

Right now is the only
situation to ever happen
at this hill, in the awkward
history of proposals.

36. proposals

There is but one true romantic spot to propose to someone in town, and that would be the hill with a white willow on top. No one knows who planted the tree. But, the saying goes that if you confess your undying love to your partner on the hill, then the both of you would be together forever.

It's very private. If you go at the right moment you can catch the flower petals falling down, raining over you in the soft breeze. Though this hill is very private, tons of people still know of its existence. Right now is the only situation to ever happen at this hill, in the awkward history of proposals.

One couple lays on the hill picnic style. The breeze is just right, it's not too hot, and there's a sort of romantic feel in the air; marriage is on the horizon for these two. They're lifelong friends who have been boyfriend/girlfriend for about four years today. He gets up and pulls her to her feet. They sway with the breeze for a bit and as they look into each other's eyes, he gets down on one knee.

"Baby, you have been with me from the beginning and I love you. I want to spend the rest of my life with you and I don't want to waste another second without you." He reaches for his pocket and pulls out a ring box.

But, before he can say those four faithful words, a couple comes rushing out to the tree laughing. They stop when they see the man on his knees and the woman staring at them too.

"Oh, my gosh." The couple says when they see the man on his knees.

"We're so sorry," the man starts, but both couples were starting to overlap each other.

The man still on his knees and his at-the-moment girlfriend, still standing over him.

"Could you guys give us a second and we'll be out of your hair?" The man on his knee says.

"No man, go ahead. Take your time," the guy responds back, then he looks at his own girlfriend, "Actually we can find another spot."

His girlfriend grips his arm.

"But, honey. I'd really like to stay here," she looks towards the couple, "This is where we first met," she explains.

"You're joking," says the almost fiancé, "This was where our first date was too."

"Hey, great minds think alike," both men say.

There's too long of a pause, so the couple standing up excuse themselves to the other side of the tree and set up their picnic as quietly as possible.

"Right," says the man on his now aching

knee, "Ruby, will you marry me?"

"Yes," she says, pulling him up. The ring finally on her finger as they share a kiss. The other couple silently cheering from their side of the tree, then gets up to meet them on their side.

"Congrats Mr. And Mrs.," the girlfriend says.

"Yea, thanks. Well, we can leave now," the fiancé says.

"What no, we won't be loud, and wow. This is awkward, but could we borrow your bottle opener?" The boyfriend says.

The newly engaged couple gives the bottle opener. Then heading back to their side and trying to quietly talk while the other couple goes on their date.

* * *

The rest of the night is awkward, to say the least, and both couples are on their toes. The recently engaged couple wish to leave but feel like if they do the other couple might think that they made it weird. Which it totally was.

See, the boyfriend of the other couple was gonna propose to his girlfriend too, but the other couple beat him to it.

"You know what, I'm just gonna do it," he helps his girlfriend up as the other couple peeks from around the willow, "honey, I know this is weird, like very weird, but I love you and I want you with me for the rest of my life."

He gets on one knee.

"Yes," she says, covering her mouth.

The other woman lets out a small "yay".

"Let me say it," he says, smiling.

"It'll still be yes," she says, jumping into his open arms. She knocks him back down, kissing his face as tears stream down her own.

The other couple cheers as the other engaged party kiss each other. They congratulate one another, then decide that this can't get any more strange and move to finish their picnic together.

Both couples can confirm that after both being happily married for five years now, that was the most awkward thing they've ever done.

Well, that and their double wedding.

THE FARMERS

She would never interact
with any of the farmers even
if it killed her, so it took one
of them coming to her to
propose an idea.

37. the farmers

Farmers don't get along very well in this town. One would think that they would try to become better friends, but they all have different personalities.

There are four main farmers in total. They run their fields like it's a military base and have no patience nor time for pleasantries. Farmer Debbie, for example, runs the farm between Farmer Ben and Farmer Jolene.

Every second is pure torture.

Farmer Ben has the ugliest scarecrow in possibly the entire world, and he's a pretentious wet wipe that can't tell the difference between sarcasm and sincerity. He grows corn, one of the biggest crops in America next to tobacco. His farm out of all of them is the most popular around the fall and Halloween season.

Farmer Jolene on the other hand is the one who grows tobacco and rye. She's a party girl who likes to smoke all day and talks like someone's covering her ears. She's not as bad as Farmer Ben but certainly is louder.

Being between them is probably the worst thing that has happened to Farmer Debbie. Her husband would joke that her being married to him was a headache. She'd call him stupid, but end up flustered in the end.

He died though, and even when she said she hated him, every second of him near her gave her a foot on her sanity.

She really loved him, but after he died the rumors started that she killed him. Though that tarnished her reputation as a person, she was still able to make due because people enjoy apples. So, she let them think that she was a husband-killing-witch. As long as she was still making a living, she'd let them believe whatever they wanted.

Farmer Debbie, stubborn as she is, will admit that she is starting to work on a friendship or rather a partnership with a certain neighbor. She would never interact with any of the farmers even if it killed her, so it took one of them coming to her to propose an idea.

* * *

She's sitting on her porch looking over the field, her cat on her lap, and the cool crisp breeze of fall in the air. This was Debbie's happy place, and a loud barking and growling kick her out of it. A golden retriever comes barreling down the dirt path leading up to her farm. Her cat spots this and makes a run for it as the dog shoots past her.

"What in the hell?" Debbie pops up and grabs her shotgun at her side.

"Whoa there Deb, no need to light up your

field on my account," a voice says from down the dirt path.

The figure gets closer, and by the strut alone, Debbie knows who it is. Farmer Jolene. No mistaking it, she has her legs crossing over one another with her dusty brown cowboy boots and straw hat. She was always wearing some color ribbon on her hat to match her checkered shirts.

"What do you want?" Debbie demands more than asks.

She lowers the barrel but doesn't put it down.

"I came all the way over here to talk business," Jolene says, sauntering over towards her porch.

"Great way to start. Call off your mutt or I'll put a bullet in him if he touches my cat."

"I won't take too long. I just want to propose an idea that could benefit both of us."

Jolene glances over at her dog, whistling real high, and shouting "down."

Debbie looks back to where the mutt and her cat ran off, and the barking stops and turns more into a whine. Debbie, satisfied that the dog won't move, sits down and waits for Jolene's pitch.

"Alright now," Jolene hops up the porch, plopping down in the rocking chair next to her, "so my idea is that it's October, right? Halloween is coming up, and rye is in season."

"Okay," Debbie says, resting her hat lower on her head.

"So are apples," Jolene says, rocking back and kicking her boots up on the railing.

"What are you proposing, Jolene? Don't beat around the bush here with me, just spit it out."

"Fine, alright. You got the apples and I got the buzz and brew. How about we team up and make some hard apple cider?" She finishes, throwing her arms out in a showman's way. Tadda.

"Hmm," Debbie murmurs under her hat.

She looks as if she's asleep.

"Oh come on, stubborn as a bull. I know you've thought of it before, you're smart, and you take risks. I know you're thinking of something else in that noggin' of yours." Jolene crosses her arms in a pout.

This idea wasn't bad, but working with Jolene might be.

"How can I trust you?" She looks over at Jolene finally, "how do I know that you're gonna carry your weight?"

"Oh don't start that now. You and I have known each other for almost twenty years now. You can trust me 'cause if you fail, I fail and so on and so forth." She waves her hands, patting her pockets for something, and chuckles when she finds what she's looking for. She brings out a cigarette, crumbled, but still in good form.

Debbie watches silently, as Jolene rests it between her lips and pats around some more in her pockets.

"Oh darn, left my lighter," she says, still

patting around.

Debbie sighs out.

"Here, but don't drop it now," she hands Jolene her lighter.

"Thanks," she lights hers and looks the lighter over, "fancy lighter here, where'd ya get it from?"

"Patrick," Debbie says, looking forward to her field.

Jolene nods, looking forward too.

"How'd he die?" She asks, breathing out a puff.

"Lung cancer," she chuckles a little, "he was a big fan of your cigarettes."

She pauses, glancing at Jolene who's staring at her.

"It wasn't your cigarettes that killed him. Something his father passed on to him that didn't mix too well with smoking." She shrugs, rocking back and forth.

"Darn," Jolene says quietly at her side.

They don't speak, but rather rock next to each other. And for the first time in a long time, Farmer Debbie felt a little better.

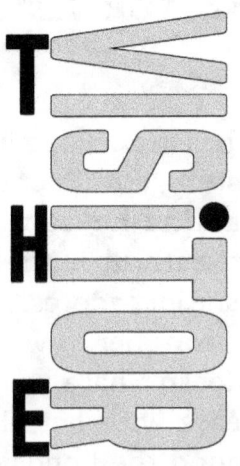

THE VISITOR

Lucinda thought that would
be the last time, but they
kept coming back...

38. the visitor

Lucinda has been living in the yellow house with the green shingles for not too long.

It's a beautiful house with two bedrooms and a large white bathtub in the center of the main bathroom that she just adores.

She lives on her own and she likes it that way. She doesn't hate people, but she gains comfort and peace with herself. Her nieces love visiting her around the holidays. She joins them for ice skating, sleigh rides, and then takes the longest bath to warm herself up.

Her sisters, however, get concerned saying she shouldn't live alone. They all live together now and have been trying for years to get Lucinda to join them. She shoos them off saying that she doesn't need to be treated like a porcelain doll. Though she hates to admit it, she misses them and it can be lonely here sometimes.

* * *

She's reading in the study when she heard the doorbell.

"Now who could that be?" She asks, getting up, and shuffling over towards the front door.

She opens it to see a young woman next to an older man in a wheelchair.

"Oh, good morning," she says to the both of them.

A look of concern and question passes her face because she's never seen them before in her life.

"Hello, Ms. Giovani. It's a pleasure to finally meet you," says the young woman.

"Oh dear, you must have me mistaken, I'm no...," she trails off as the woman hands her a notepad.

It reads. "Please pretend that you are Ms. Giovani, I'll explain later."

"Oh.., I mean. Dear, the pleasure's all mine. Won't you come in?" She holds the door open wide.

Maybe she does this out of curiosity, boredom, and because she has been getting into her mysteries lately.

"Thank you," the lady leans down towards the old man's ear, "we're going into her house and you haven't said a thing."

The older man looks down at his wrinkled hands and then looks forward to where Lucinda would be.

"Uh, good morning," he says shyly.

"Good morning," she says, as the woman pushes him in.

They all head into the study, while the young woman sits the man right next to the chair Lucinda was in.

"Uh, would you all like some tea?" Lucinda tries her best to calm her nerves. It's been forever since anyone has visited her.

"I'll take coffee if you have any," the man says.

"Certainly, and you dear?" She turns to the woman adjusting the man's coat.

"Oh please, call me Selena. And let me help you."

Selena and Lucinda walk over to the kitchen. Once Selena closes the door, she explains.

"I'm so sorry for intruding in your house like this, but my patient Frankie asked to be brought here. He claims that his friend Grace used to live here."

"Well I'm sorry dear, but she either moved away or she passed. I've been here for almost four years now."

"I had a feeling, but he was so sure that she was still here."

She nods, as Lucinda grabs a few mugs for the coffee and tea.

"He's blind and can't tell what you look like, but I understand that this is a lot to ask of you, so you don't have to do it. I just couldn't say no to him. He really is a sweet man. I can make up an excuse and you won't have to see us again though." Selena finishes, chewing at her nails.

Lucinda looks at her sweetly. Such a passionate and kind girl that she is willing to make this man feel better.

Lying, but still sweet.

"That won't be necessary Selena. I'll help."

Selena smiles back at her and together they take the coffee and tea into the room. Lucinda takes Frankie's hand gently and gives him the coffee cup. He looks at where she'd be and reaches for her hand too.

"Thank you Grace," he says.

"My pleasure Frankie," she says softly, sitting across from him still holding his open hand.

"You'll have to forgive me earlier. I was afraid that you wouldn't remember me." He takes a slow sip.

"That's alright dear. At our age you can't be too sure," she laughs with him.

✽ ✽ ✽

Lucinda thought that would be the last time, but they kept coming back and she didn't mind one bit. Lucinda and Frankie "caught up" while Selena sat and watched. She'd sometimes fill in the blanks Lucinda couldn't "remember". It made her feel alive. She never realized how much she's actually been lonely and in need of people until they showed up in her life.

"Coming, coming," Lucinda says, walking towards the door. She colored her lips today and curled her hair, even though he couldn't see her.

"My, my Ms. Giovani. You look hot," Selena

says, pushing in Frankie.

"Oh stop," she looks over at Frankie, taking his free hand in hers.

"You got dolled up just for me," he smirks, which looks quite handsome on him. In his other hand are a bouquet of flowers.

"Ha, you wish," she flirts back, "Are those for me?" She gasps.

"Ha, you wish," he copies back and they all laugh.

They head to the study again, where they usually meet. Selena takes the flowers to the kitchen. Lucinda has had so much fun with these two, the most fun in weeks. She turns her head back to face Frankie, as he smiles sweetly in her direction. A sad smile passes her, and if only he could see her. He would tell that she's a liar by her eyes.

It's been fun, but she can't trick him anymore. She can't play pretend anymore, not with Frankie. She has to tell him that his dear Grace doesn't live here anymore, that she hasn't been here in over four years. He deserves to know the truth, even if that means she can't see him ever again.

"Frankie, dear. There's something I have to tell you." She squeezes his hand softly.

"You aren't my Grace, are you?" He asks, but he doesn't sound mad or even remotely upset. He actually has a silly grin on his face, as if he had something to confess to her.

"Uh, how did you know?"

"An old friend told me about her moving away about five years ago, after our first visit." He shrugs like it's nothing.

"Oh, Frankie. You must be so mad. I'm sorry it's gone on so long," Lucinda says, looking away, and pulling her hand back.

"I'm not," he reaches out his hand for her.

She hesitates but takes it. His grip is firm in her hands

"You may not be my Grace, but you are so much more. We've talked more, you're so kind, and I can tell by your voice that you are very beautiful," he says, smiling, "I was lonely too and going to dark places. Grace was my only hope at the time, but you are the one that saved me."

"Lucinda is my real name," she says shyly.

"Lucinda, so very nice to meet you," he brings her hand to his lips.

"Oh Frankie, stop," she says as Selena comes back.

She laughs as Lucinda covers her burning cheeks and Frankie wiggles his eyebrows at her.

Listen Dude. I hate to break it to you, but I'm a dude and I think this girl gave you the wrong number

39. wrong number

Wassup ;)

That's the text that John receives after he gets off from working at the Drive-in Theater.

He doesn't recognize the number. He's tired and very cautious after the whole "I talked to a murderer and didn't die incident", so he sends a simple text.

Wrong Number

Not thinking too much about it once he gets home and about to eat his very late dinner does he hear his phone. Rummaging around the couch, he checks his phone.

"Crap," he says under his breath. He forgot to block the number.

This ain't the wrong number girl
I know you gave me the digits

Listen Dude

I hate to break it to you but...

I'm a dude

and I think this girl gave you the wrong

number

John puts his phone down thinking that was the end of it again.

Prove it

This dude is relentless. John scoops some food in his mouth while he thinks of a response to cut him loose.

Excuse me

Send a picture that proves you ain't a girl

and I'll leave you b

I am not doing that

That's creepy, man

How do I know you aren't a pervert?

You right tho

The number sends a picture of who John assumes is texting him. Shrugging, John sends a picture so ugly this guy won't even think about stalking him. He hits send and not even two seconds later are there two messages.

Yo
You white as hell

Thanks, I guess

Nah, my bad

You just look
scrunched

                           Just being safe

               in case you want to eat my brains or
                                  something

Woah Woah. I ain't no zombie or Hannibal

                 You watch the silence of the lambs?

Movie is a masterpiece

      They ended up talking all night. John sends him a better picture and the guy replies he still looks white as hell. This makes John laugh out loud.

      He finds out that this dude wants to be a director, his name is Gavin, and he has a pug named Madame Butterfly. He sends a picture of her. John smiles, wishing he had a pet to send back to Gavin.

You know I almost forgot why I texted you in the first
place

                    You thought I was a girl

That's right
You'd be the ugliest girl dawg

              I'm taking that as a compliment

Straight up compliment.

Hey, I gotta head to bed

I got a long day tomorrow

Word

I gotta new job

Hey, Congrats man

Thanks

I like working, keeps my mind sharp ya know

You got no idea

Goodnight man

You too

That was the longest and nicest conversation John's had in a long time. He cleans up his food and climbs into bed. He rolls around not being able to fall asleep now, then grabs his phone and decides to save Gavin's number.

CO WORKERS

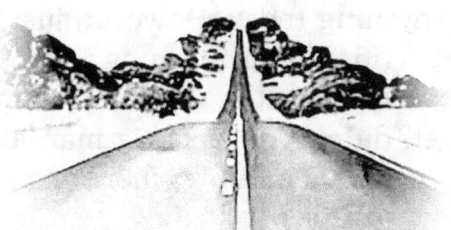

"Yea, there was a slip up
with my room assignment.
Glad to be among friends,"
he jokes.

40. co-workers

It was a mix-up in the halls. He wasn't the only teacher out of place in the school, but it certainly was the oddest placement. He's a math teacher, ranging from Algebra to Calculus, but he was accidentally placed in the language hall.

"If I screw up, all they have to do is talk smack to me in a different language." He says, taking his lunch break.

It was the first Monday back to school. So far his classes were fine as he didn't really have to teach anything today. However, just the walk down the corridor in the morning and it seems the teachers can smell that he's fresh meat.

"Well didn't you take German all of high school?" His fellow math teacher tries to counsel him.

"Yea, but even if I wanted to hold a conversation it's like it won't matter. I'm the freshman in this case and they're the seniors." He shivers at a memory from his high school days.

* * *

The next few days went fine. His class started working on Wednesday, and the students so far didn't seem to despise his guts.

"Alright everybody, we're gonna start a new activity at the end of the day that I made up last night."

He claps to wake them up.

"It's called lightning round, so get into groups, no more than five. When I show a part of the syllabus or a formula we learned today. You write it on your whiteboards and hold it up. I'll take the quickest group, so work together. In the end, I'll tally up how many points you get and add it on to your next quiz or test."

They scattered and were ready in seconds. Soon after, things were getting loud and by the end of the day the kids rang up a lot of points.

"Alright, get out of here and enjoy the sun," he says, dismissing them as the bell rings, "we'll discuss where you want these points to go on Friday."

He waits by the door and watches them go.

After the halls were nearly empty, and he was about to turn in to pack up. The teachers surrounded him, like vultures swarming in for the easy pickings.

"I've been meaning to introduce myself. My name is Jerome Fischer. I teach math, " he says nervously, sticking out his hand for anyone to shake.

They all look at his hand like it's a dead rat, so he slowly lowers it.

"Listen Jerome," one teacher, who he

assumes is one of the French teachers, catches his attention, "Your class was very loud today and we all would appreciate it if you didn't get them so loud."

"Yep, that's my bad," he says, hands up in surrender now.

"We understand it is a mistake that you are here, but do not make this hall your zoo, si?" A shorter woman says up to him.

"Got it, no noise," he says, trying to hold back a smart remark.

They all turn to leave and head back to their own rooms. He breathes out a sigh and rubs his face, a woman was still on his left; it's the teacher next door. He read her sign, laughing a little 'cause it's German. Real funny, he thinks as he makes his way over to her.

"Um, I'm sorry. You must have gotten the most out of my classes loudness."

"It's alright," she says, "They really gave you a mouthful, no?" She nods over to the other teachers.

"Yea, but I guess I was bound to slip up," he shrugs, leaning against the doorframe, "I guess today was just that day."

"I understand your feelings," she points at herself, "I am new too."

"Ahh, fellow fresh meat," he stretches his hand out and she actually takes it to shake, "Jerome Fisher."

"Mariam Heinz," she shakes his hand, "it is

strange that you are not a language teacher," she says, leaning against her own door to match him.

"Yea, there was a slip up with my room assignment. Glad to be among friends," he jokes, "you know, I actually took German back in high school?"

She looks surprised, then she leans forward as if to say prove it. He laughs again, thinking of what to say.

"Hallo Mariam, wie geht es dir?"

"Gut" she nods back approvingly, "Your German is very good" she smiles finally.

"I know it's a surprise that a black guy speaks German right?"

She laughs, knocking her head back as if he's said the funniest thing.

"No, there are plenty of black people in Germany." She says bluntly.

It was his turn to laugh back. She opens her door wide enough to invite him in.

"Where in Germany are you from?" He sits at a desk across from her.

From that point on, until he got to his official room, they talked every day and ate lunch together in each other's rooms. Even when he did get his new room and ten years later, they were still the best of friends.

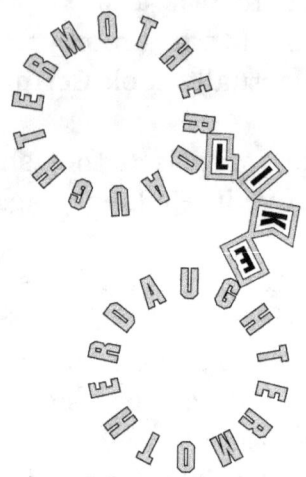

"I got a call from the prison today. She's gonna be released tomorrow."

41. like mother like daughter

She nearly drops her fork on the plate. Wants to, but that would've made her jump even more.

"I'm sorry, what did you say?" Tanisha's Grandma asks, slowly resting her fork down.

"I got a call from the prison today. She's gonna be released tomorrow."

"Oh." So her hearing wasn't failing her.

"Yea, and I was wondering if I could pick her up? I don't have to go alone. I could take—" Tanisha tries slowly.

"No, that's out of the question."

"But Grandma."

"No, if she wants to find her way home there's the city bus," she says sternly.

Her granddaughter stares hard at her plate, refusing to meet her eyes now. Tanisha still loves her mother, goes to visit her a few times, and sends her letters. She's getting close to her mother's age when things went from bad to worse.

"Baby, listen. I don't mean to be snappy with you, it's just I don't know what she'll do."

"I know. I've been thinking about it too," she says, looking up.

"You do?"

"Yea, I wonder if I have it sometimes. You know, I'm getting close to the age when she had me." Tanisha says, messing with her napkin now, " I remember bits and pieces when I was young. Selling pineapples on the road, holding her hair back, and lots of broken glass. I wonder every day if I'll be like her." She finishes.

Her grandmother stares at her granddaughter. Tanisha knows so much and thinks so hard. She never knew that her baby, her sweet Tanisha, was afraid that she'd end up like her mother.

"Oh honey, I didn't know you felt this way. You will never be like her, "she reaches across the table to hold her hand and Tanisha grips her back.

That was all the answer she could give her, no reassurance but a command.

"I know. It's just a scary thought. I know I'll never be that way," she shifts in her chair, "I can't be that way. I just can't."

"Yea," her grandma says, a smile on her face now.

She's proud of herself for raising this one right. Good school, studying together, lots of reading and her friends are good. She's into sports and as far as she knows, no boyfriend.

She's proud, but thinking about her own daughter now a sad thought passes her. Could she have done anything differently? Could she have done something sooner to prevent this?

"Do you ever miss her?" Tanisha meets her

Grandma's eyes.

"Sometimes," she admits.

"Yea, me too," her granddaughter agrees.

* * *

She thinks back to when Tanisha was young, maybe too young to remember. There were days that she'd come over to her house with her mother late at night.

Her granddaughter was barely standing in her little pajamas looking worn out. Her bouncing mother is the complete opposite bringing her over to the kitchen.

"Hey ma, you got any tater tots, my little worker bee is hungry," she'd pick up Tanisha and buzz her around the kitchen. Tanisha would give out a laugh and wave her arms around to fly.

"No, not since the last time you were here." She said plainly.

Wrapped in her robe, she took Tanisha from her hands and sat her in the dining room chair. She busied herself around the kitchen for some bread and sandwich fixings.

"Hey ma, would you mind if we crash here for a bit, the house is fine. It's just—"

"Yes, you can stay," she'd cut her off.

"Okay, thanks," she said, hopping off the counter.

A loud bang hit the table, as Tanisha had fallen asleep, popped up, and grabbed at her forehead.

Later on that night, Tanisha slept in the guest room when her mom got up. She tucked the covers back around Tanisha and snuck out of the room. She crept down the hall and grabbed her boots along the way.

"Where're you going?" Tanisha's Grandma waited in a chair for this very moment.

"Out." Her daughter said as she pulled on her boots.

"The hell you are. Get back in bed with your daughter before I kick you back there myself."

"Mom, I'm going for a smoke. I'll be back in a flash."

"If you walk out that door now, then you sure as hell aren't welcome back." She put her foot down.

She looked at her mom for a long time, then opened the door and left. Two weeks later they found her hiding in the basement of the library.

❊ ❊ ❊

"It's a miracle you turned out alright," she says, now putting away the dishes while Tanisha washes them.

"Well, I had you," she says with a smile, "thank you." Tanisha bends to kiss her forehead.

Her grandma squeezes her tight, then gets back to work. Yeah, her daughter's sorry ass can take the bus back to another place, because what she said was true. She ain't welcome back here in this house.

...sometimes it's hard to
find the things you love
more than the things
you hate.

42. love on repeat

Love is one of the greatest tools in the toolbox of life, but people don't like to talk about love too much. Not in a bad way, but sometimes it's hard to find the things you love more than the things you hate. It's easier to hate than it is to love. But love is still a powerful thing, it can heal, unite, and create beautiful things. Glenndale learned what it truly means to love. They started to understand their own type of love, and nothing like being cramped in a town shows that.

* * *

The whole town, from the oldest Librarian all the way to the children, were sitting in the field. It's dark and cold, but some people brought lanterns, flashlights, and heavy blankets to keep them warm. They all looked calm, everyone huddling up with friends and family just watching the stars.

A lone boy was resting on a blanket by himself wearing her hoodie.

"Hey, I know it's been some time since you've been gone, but this beautiful night reminds me of you. You and I would sit out here when it was warmer though," he chuckles a little, huddling further in the hoodie for warmth, " I understand that I have to let you go. It's taken me seeing the same day over and over to realize that. I really miss you and I love you," he says, a tear rolling down his face as a figure joins him on the grass.

"Mind if I join?" She asks.

"Not at all." He makes room for the Mayor.

She looks at him and without a word wraps her arm over his shoulder. They lean into each other in silence.

It's close to midnight once again. The parents let their kids stay out with them, wrapping them in the tightest hugs this night. Kids for the longest time in forever, hugging them back. Friends lean into each other, all off their phones, and just looking up at the stars.

"You know I couldn't ask for a better group."

"Oh stop Viv, don't get all Samuel L. Jackson *Deep Blue Sea* with me," Morgan says at her side.

"Don't encourage her, she'll try to do his voice," one of the twins says.

Vivian gets up and starts to do her best Samuel L. Jackson impression. They all laugh at her and get up to dance around. Morgan and Allison grabbing hands, spinning around while Darren picks up Vivian and spins her around. The twins race over to their mom and grab her to join. Soon after, everyone in town is up and dancing to no beat in particular. They all chant and dance, grabbing their neighbors and pulling them close.

"Mind if I have this dance?" Alex asks Tanisha.

She takes his hand and they sway. The crowd swirling around them while they lean into one another. Her head resting on his shoulder, then she lifts her head up and grabs Alex's face to pull him into a kiss. He holds her tight and kisses her back.

As the clock strikes midnight signaling November 8th, the clock restarts and it's November 7th all over again.

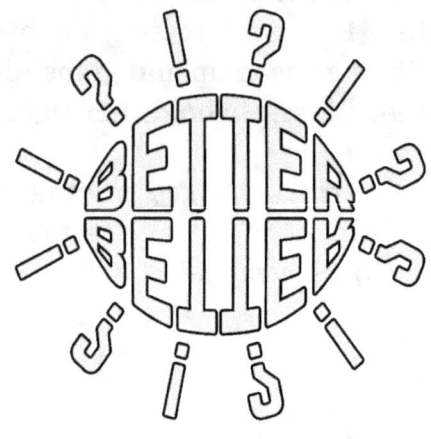

"Better! Do you think abandoning her is for better?"

43. better?!

Sitting across from her granddaughter and thinking of the right things to say is one of the hardest things she's ever done.

Tanisha woke up at around eight, asking where her mommy was. Probably off to the store or to a friend's house baby girl, she had lied through her teeth. They spent the entire day distracting one another from Tanisha's mom.

They went to the library, got ice cream, even went to a jazz concert in town. It's dinner time now and that's where she's blanking. Trying to think of what to say to ease Tanisha's mind.

"Grandma, grandma." Tanisha shook her sleeves.

She had probably called her name a dozen times.

"Yes, sorry baby."

"Where's mommy?" Tanisha asked once again.

She thought of anything, anything at all. Just a good enough lie until she can find Tanisha's good-for-nothing mother.

"She's getting you your most favorite book, sugar. It's really far away, though."

"Ohhh," Tanisha nods her head as if

figuring out a puzzle, "she's getting me the Secret Of Rain Cavalier?"

"Yes baby, and she won't be back for a while. That's why she dropped you off here."

"Ohhh," she said, smiling at last, "Cool. Thanks, Grandma."

"No problem baby. Are you done?"

Tanisha nodded, and she put their dishes in the sink and helped clean up the kitchen. By the time they're done, did she realize that tomorrow is Monday. Tanisha has to go back to school.

"When does your mama send you to bed?"

"I get in bed around eight." She wiped her hands on the towel after stacking a glass to dry.

"You need help getting ready?"

"No ma'am, I'm good," she said, then walked off, and grabbed a towel from the hall closet to shower.

She waited for Tanisha to start the shower then rushed to her room. She dialed the number. No answer. Again, no answer. She tried five more times before she got an answer.

"Who the hell is this?" She said to the voice who clearly wasn't her daughter.

"Uh, sorry. I thought this was my phone," he said.

"Hand this phone to Corey."

She heard him yell for Corey.

"Yo," she said.

"Get. Home. Right. Now."

"I should've known, listen Ma—"

"No, you listen to me. I didn't sacrifice everything in my life just for you to do this to your own daughter, so you better come back right now. She needs her mother. She needs stability." She said as quietly as possible, but still tried to scold.

"And you think I can provide that for her? Mom, I'm a screwup and I want her to have better."

"Better! Do you think abandoning her is for better?" She asked, looking around for a smart answer.

"I left her to you. I know you won't screw her up after taking on me."

"Corey..." she said, pinching the bridge of her nose.

"Listen Ma," she started, but screaming and a siren in the background took over, "I have to go, give her a kiss for me please."

The line went dead, as she sat down hard on the bed. The little pitter-patters of Tanisha's feet came into her room. She had her little pj's on and a book in her hand.

"Can I sleep with you, Grandma?"

"Of course honey, come here," she opened her arms and Tanisha crawled in. She opened her book and read. Soon after they both fell asleep.

* * *

The next day, while Tanisha was at school. She headed to the bookstore looking for the book.

"Hi, I'm looking for the secret life of Rain something."

"Oh Rain Cavalier, I think we have a few in the back." The woman said, cheerfully.

"Thanks."

She waited, then perked when she overheard two women.

"The cops busted a few of them, but some got away."

"It's a shame. I knew one of the girls from high school."

"Who?"

"You remember Corey?"

She leaned forward a little and scratched her arm to act less suspicious.

"Yea, she got our class in trouble for that one senior prank."

"A shame, but she wasn't caught, right? She's missing now."

"You're joking?"

She stared as they walked away. Missing. She's missing.

"Here you are, ma'am." The employee came back with the book.

"Oh, thanks." She turned slowly to her, or maybe it was all in slow motion.

She decided that she has to tell Tanisha. The sooner the better, she thought as she walked back home. Tanisha's smart, she'll either figure it out eventually or beg her to tell. She saw her walking home now.

"Hey baby," she said, concealing her bag.

Tanisha grumbled something but walked into the house.

"Hello, excuse me." She said, following her in.

"Hi," Tanisha said, trying not to get smart with her.

"Listen here, little miss. I understand that our situation isn't ideal, but there's no reason—"

"Mommy's missing isn't she?" Tanisha spun around on her.

She paused at her outburst.

"My friend at school told me. Told me they were busted for drugs and mommy's missing," she yelled, tears covering her face now, "did you know?!"

"Baby," she said softly.

"No, don't touch me. You lied to me. She's missing. She's missing!" She screamed, shaking all over.

She wrapped her arms around Tanisha. At first, the little girl kicked and screamed some more, but relaxed under her grip. Tanisha held her tight and cried into her grandma's arms.

"Where'd she go, is she alright?" She said through hiccups.

"I don't know honey. I don't know," she said. She squeezed her tighter.

She was the glue and the
consistent force that kept
these women at bay.

44. the falling out

It's nice to have a strong foundation for friendships. Without a strong foundation, any inconvenience can ruin the whole thing. Some people are such good friends that they don't need to know trivial things. While others would like to know the trivial things. Other people make friends with others in a hobby or common interest. However, there are some cases where a group of friends truly hate each other's guts. They only stay together for confidence and to avoid being alone.

The mayor's wife has always been friends with these ladies ever since she moved here at the beginning of high school. Before her, the girls never talked to each other, more so talked about each other than with one another.

The Mayor's Wife was the city girl back then, with whom everyone wanted to be friends. Who wouldn't? She was pretty, smart, kind, and very confident in everything that she did. The girls came together to be her friends, stamping out their pride just to get a taste of her.

Throughout the years after high school, some kept close, others left, and new people came in. However, the mayor's wife stayed at the center of it all without even knowing it. She was the glue and the consistent force that kept these women at bay. So one day when she asked if they would join her to help her run the town, they agreed despite them not really wanting to see the others.

* * *

It's been only a handful of months that they've been in politics with one another. It really put their friendship to the test.

Unlike their usual Saturday book club meetings, these ladies had to see each other almost every day. Like most cabinets, they butt heads. However, it seems that they are the only cabinet to bump heads, come to little or no agreement, and personal insults.

The Mayor's Wife decided that enough was enough, and called an important meeting at town hall rather than the library this time. She gave the Bodyguard the day off, asking him to go take the librarian on a date. He said yes so quickly and left before she could finish her sentence. The mayor's wife set up a nice spread at the center coffee table in her office. Though she had a very hard decision to make about her friends, she dressed as if to say nothing to see here.

The ladies start to trickle in. Some start to sit as far apart from one another, but as the room filled up they had no choice but to sit next to each other.

"Great, now everybody. Don't be shy. Eat up,

this is no meeting discussing politics, just catching up on our lives." She reaches for a few chips herself.

The Mayor's Wife sits down in the chair to face them all. A few ladies reach for the spread after she stares for a while. They're all quiet, but in the hidden tension kind of way, only a group of highly opinionated women can hold.

"I'll go first, so I talked to all of those twenty children and they're slowly opening up, isn't that wonderful?" The mayor's wife says while they eat.

A few people reply, but others don't say a thing.

"Okay, guys."

She sets down her plate to face them.

"We're friends and I feel like we need to hash it out so that we can do better. Not only the people we govern but ourselves as well. We need to hash it out now," she says, looking around.

"You know what, you're right. I just have to say," Tanisha's grandma starts, looking at all the other women in their eyes, "you all are truly insufferable."

And just that sentence started the whole ordeal. There was shouting, finger-pointing, and lots of standing up. All while the Mayor's Wife lets them go on like that for maybe ten minutes before standing up. She raps her gavel against her desk to get their attention.

"Alright good, it's healthy for us to fight. Sometimes friends need to fight. Now I believe that—"

"No, I'm not done," Abby White cuts her off, "Ann Marie, what is your deal with me? Don't hate on me or my child just because my house is bigger." She spits out.

"My problem is that you have been a no-good hussy since high school. It's a shame your daughter doesn't know who you really are." Ann Marie shouts back.

"Oh, she knows. And it sucks cause she won't tell me things anymore. I found out that she applied to NYU and got in!" She screams, tears forming in the corners of her eyes.

"Oh that's wonderful, right?" The mayor's wife says, hoping to diffuse the situation.

Trying to put some positivity back into the conversation.

"No it's not Joann, it means that my baby is leaving, but you'll never understand cause you don't have children." She points at the Mayor's Wife.

The room goes dead silent as the mayor's wife's smile slowly melts away. Vivian's mom starts to say something, tries to backpedal, but the mayor's wife slowly holds up her hand. She walks over to her desk and gets out a folder.

"It's true. I called you all here to hash it out, but I had another reason." She shuffles the papers out, looking at all the ladies with a serious tone in her eyes.

"When I took the position of Mayor, I fired the old and brought you all in because I wanted comfort and something familiar. I wanted my friends to help me and for us to grow closer, but I see now that it has torn us apart. That was selfish of me to uproot you all for my benefit. That's a mistake I have to live with now.

I have been interviewing new candidates for your positions," she lifts her hand one more time as the women start to get up to say something, "I mean no offense. I love you all dearly, but this and our friendships don't mix. And sometimes I feel like I'm the only one taking this whole governing stuff seriously," she admits, " I see that your hearts aren't in it as much as mine. I hadn't realized that or wanted to see it until now. I'm sorry, but as of today you all are relieved of your duties."

She leaves the pink slips on the corner of her desk. When she looks up at them, they really see that she means it and that it pains her to say it.

They knew that they weren't the best at their jobs, but they thought that maybe she'd overlook that. They should've known better than to hold her back.

They take their slips with no fuss and leave. And though the mayor's wife wants them to all still be friends, this might be the last they see each other. After all, the mayor's wife was really their glue.

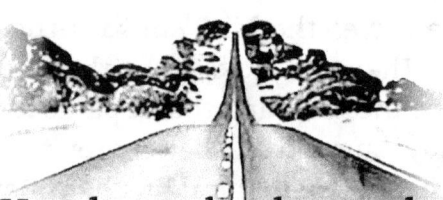

He whoops loud enough to
catch the attention of the
attendance office, so she
grabs his hand and they
both run out.

45. ditch days

She's getting a drink from the water fountain when a figure slides right behind her.

"Hey weirdo, you're invading my personal space," she says, turning around to face Roman.

"You keep hogging all the water, this is the coldest one in school," he says, playfully pushing her aside.

"You brute," she says, stepping back, but waiting for him.

After she found out that the hoodie gave her enough luck to last her forever, she decided that it's best to not get caught wearing it every day. It's in her backpack now. She was afraid to wash it for a week, but once she did, nothing happened, except perhaps her luck got better.

"So what are you doing on this ditch day?" He asks her.

"Juniors don't get ditch days, and anyways the day just started."

"Then we're late." He acts surprised, grabbing his head in exasperation.

She rolls her eyes as he steps in front of her walking backward.

"Oh you didn't hear, did you?"

"What, Roman?" She plays along.

"Today is a school-wide ditch day, of course. Word didn't get around, it just made news yesterday."

"Is that why you don't have a backpack this morning?"

"Exactly. You look like you don't believe me, come look."

He takes her to the woodshop class.

"See, only one girl is in there and that's cause she's crazy about taking days off and perfect attendance." He shrugs like it's a known fact.

"Okay, that does say something, but what about the call for the assembly not too long ago?"

"Oh Mari, that's for the freshmen. They're our distraction. And they don't deserve a ditch day, they made it through one year, big deal."

She laughs but lets him pull her towards the exit.

"Whaddaya say, wanna ditch with me?"

She looks at the front office, all eyes on either a book or the computer screen. She shrugs.

"Why not?"

He whoops loud enough to catch the attention of the attendance office, so she grabs his hand and they both run out. Giggling they run towards his car, driving off, and still laughing as she looks over at him smiling.

* * *

Their ditch day was awesome. They went to

233

the end of the school year carnival, got lots of fried food and a huge jug of lemonade to wash it down. They each won the other a stuffed animal, rode on the Ferris wheel, and then made their way to the top of the hill with the willow tree. It was close to school getting out by the time they got there.

She pulls out her hoodie and uses it as a pillow.

"Today was so much fun," she says, lying back looking at the branches swaying in the breeze.

"Yea, it was." He scoots up next to her on the hoodie.

"Today wasn't a ditch day was it?"

"Nope." He laughs as she hits his sides.

"I figured, but why?"

"Well," he says turning on his side to face her, "I've known you since we were kids and I've always seen you so caught up in your head. I've always wondered what's inside that pretty head of yours."

"Well thank you." She blushes.

"For what?"

"Getting me out. You know sometimes I feel so unlucky."

"Like the time you turned Peter gay?" He smiles, trying to avoid another punch.

"He was like that when I kissed him," she says, punching his side anyway.

He grabs her fist, pulling her closer.

"The point is that I've always felt so

unlucky, but then things got better, once I opened my mouth and ran into you."

"When I ran into you, you mean. Oh, and that day I was lying," he says, lacing one of her hands into his, "I knew your name. I just wanted an excuse to touch your hand."

She smiles before pushing him back.

"Gross, you weirdo," she says, laughing, and he laughs too as they lean into each other. She thanks her lucky stars for this hoodie and grabbing his hand back, hoping he never let go.

THE ONE STILL WHO LIES

"What happened is that you lied to me."

46. the one who lies still

She didn't want it to be true. She couldn't allow it to be true.

She was going through the mail when she saw a letter addressed to Vivian. She never gets mail from anyone except for her taxes or from her father, so what could it be?

It was from NYU. At first, she was pissed because how could Vivian apply out of state without telling her. Then she calmed down. Vivian couldn't get into NYU. Not saying her daughter wasn't smart. No, rather she just couldn't imagine it.

That was her dream school. The one thing she and Vivian share. It's also the school she got waitlisted for and had to settle for a community college in town. Joann got into NYU. And though she doesn't hate her for it, sometimes when they were younger she wished Jo got expelled out from there.

She decided to open the letter just to calm her nerves. The envelope was kinda thick, not a good sign already. She pulled out the paper and read it aloud.

"Dear Vivian White, we'd first like to congratulate you on making us one of your picks.

We'd like to welcome you—" she stops herself short.

She read it over again. Over and over again. Vivian got in. She got into New York University.

The front door opens and slams shut. She grabs the rest of her mail and heads to her office, sitting behind her computer but not turning it on.

"Hey," Vivian says, swinging into the room.

Her beautiful daughter. She's got her blonde hair clipped back to show her beautiful brown eyes. She was brilliant and terrifying, and so wonderful. She should be shouting from the rooftops that her daughter got into her dream school, but the words wouldn't come out. Fear held tight on her throat.

"Don't slam the doors."

She tries to move her mail around and shifts Vivian under her own, but Vivian catches her move.

"Any mail for me?"

"Nope," she says, shaking her head, "You expecting any?" She decides to change tactics and turns it to her.

Why did she go behind my back for New York? Why didn't she tell me?

"Well, I applied early for some colleges, so they'd send a letter," Vivian answers smoothly.

"Yep, well nothing yet." She lies.

❋ ❋ ❋

That was the end of it, or so she thought. A few days after Halloween, she was given the boot at work after Joann thought it was a good time to grow a pair. Good for her. It's about time Joann put them all in their place.

She's watching some trashy tv show when the door opens and slams the door.

"Vivian, we do not slam doors, that's mahogany dear."

"Mom," she says. She walks in front of her, a sort of fire in her eyes.

"What happened?"

"What happened is that you lied to me."

"About what?" She asks, sitting up now. It can only be about NYU.

"NYU, mom. I did get an acceptance letter, didn't I?" She didn't wait for a response, 'cause she already knew, "ugh, this is so like you."

"Like me? I didn't hear anything about going to New York from you." She throws her arms up.

"How could I when I knew you'd react like this?"

"Oh, so it's wrong to care about my daughter?" She crosses her arms.

"It's not that mom and you know it," Vivian screams, "stop trying to gaslight me! You know why I applied," she points at her.

"'Cause it's your dream school, I know Viv. I know, but we talked about applying in-state!" She screams back just as loud.

Their dog staring up at them in confusion.

"Oh, so you do pay attention?" Vivian asks, crossing her arms just as she had done.

"Well, why wouldn't I huh?"

"Mom, even if I didn't want to go, and even if I got rejected. You already made the decision for me. If you had told me. We would have talked, maybe we would've argued, but if you had heard things from my side we wouldn't be in this situation. I had to hide this from you 'cause you want to keep me in this little bubble and I can't take it anymore." She grips her hair like she used to do when she was young and ready to throw a tantrum.

"Oh, cut the crap Vivian. When were you really gonna tell me?" She nods her head, "right, never. 'Cause we never talk anymore. Never tell each other anything."

"Cause you never listen. It took you forever to understand that I wanted to write. You wouldn't listen when I dropped out of soccer, and you aren't listening now. Mom, why is it so hard for you to understand that?" She crosses and uncrosses her arms.

"Oh no. Upstairs now!" She points.

Vivian stomps halfway up the stairs before turning around.

"Oh and I would've found out about it anyway 'cause they send emails!" She screams, running the rest of the way up.

She sits back down, covering her eyes. That

was their worst fight, and it's not like this hasn't happened before. The lies still go on, and none of them refuse or know how to break the cycle.

THE DETECTOR

She turns to Jackie, so does
the whole room as she
checks the machine, not
meeting their eyes.

47. the lie detector

"Come on guys. I swear we won't get in trouble," the boyfriend says.

"Easy for you to say, man. If you get busted you won't go to jail," his best friend says next to him, helping him carry it over to the basement table.

The girls follow them in, sitting down on the beanbag chair, and watching them set it up. Once they're done, the boyfriend turns around and flashes his brightest smile towards the girls.

"Alright ladies, who's going first?"

"Do you really think that any of us will go first?" His girlfriend asks, looking at the others for confirmation.

"Alright, I'll go first," Jackie says, standing up and walking over.

"Of course she goes first," the girl next to the girlfriend mumbles under her breath.

The guys hook her up and the girlfriend tenses as her boyfriend linger around Jackie's stomach to hook the wire to her. Jackie just looks forward and takes calming breaths.

"Come on Jackie Jacks, it shouldn't be too hard unless you're hiding something," the best friend says.

"I'm an open book Troy, you can look through my pages anytime," she winks.

"Right, so how do we do this thing?" The girlfriend stands up to join her boyfriend.

"Well, I'm the only one who knows how to work it. Anyone can ask her a question and I'll tell you if she's telling the truth or not," he looks at Jackie, "Ready?"

"Yup."

He gestures for anyone to ask.

"Is it true that you got pregnant and had to give the baby away?" The girl looks away from her phone to ask.

"Wow," Troy says with a nervous laugh.

Jackie looks over at her, and the room shifts to a state of tensed silence as she answers.

"No, I was never pregnant. Even if I was, I would never give the baby away."

They pause, waiting for the confirmation.

"She's telling the truth," the boyfriend says.

The one who asked the question has to look away and goes back to her phone instead.

"Is it true that you like me, Jackie O?" Troy says, leaning towards her.

"Ew no," she says.

"Lie." The boyfriend laughs.

"Alright alright, you're cute and I do like you as a friend." She pats his hand with a smile on her face.

"I'll take it," he says, fist-pumping in the air.

"Come on guys hit me with something

hard," she says, flexing her fingers.

"What about Theo?" The girlfriend points at her boyfriend.

"What about him?"

"Have you ever thought about him?" She asks.

"Well yeah, he's my friend."

"That's true," Theo says.

"No, you know what I mean," the girlfriend challenges Jackie.

"Oh, you mean romantically. Well yea, here and there, but I'm not a homewrecker," Jackie says, meeting her gaze head-on.

"Truth," Theo says quietly.

There's another pause, this one somehow tenser than before.

"Welp, I've done enough confession, you're up Theo," Jackie says, unhooking.

"I can't, I'm the only one—"

"Well, I've been watching enough crime shows to know how to work it."

"Honestly—"

"No, she's right. What do you have to hide?" The girlfriend nods to him.

He looks between her and Jackie.

"I promise I won't break it," Jackie says, hands up.

"Fine, fine whatever," he says, hooking himself up.

"Alright, man. I'll start you off nice and easy," Troy says, "Did you put a little dent in the back of my car?"

"That's nice and easy?" He coughs out a laugh.

"Listen, I'm not mad, but I just wanna know cause I got a beating and a half for it."

"No dude, I swear. Your sister ran her bike into it and begged me not to tell you. You saw me back out cause I was passing by when I saw it happen."

They all look towards Jackie.

"Truth."

"Alright, thanks, man." Troy says, clapping his shoulder, "glad I can count on you, kinda," he hits him a little harder.

"Do you like Jackie?" His girlfriend asks next.

"Yes."

"Truth," Jackie says, checking the machine.

"Romantically?"

"No."

"It's true," Jackie says, eyes down.

"Have you kissed her before?"

"Yes, but—"

"Is it true Jackie?" She spins to face her.

"Isn't he the one hooked up?" She tries to laugh a little, but it falls flat.

"I wanna hear it from you?" The girlfriend stands near her.

"Yes, we did kiss, but listen," Jackie gets up from the chair, "listen okay, there was a time before you two dated, so yes we kissed."

She turns towards Theo, ready to kick him if he lies.

"When?" She demands.

"Seventh grade, it was spin the bottle." Theo answers.

She turns to Jackie, so does the whole room as she checks the machine, not meeting their eyes.

"It's true."

❋ ❋ ❋

They returned the machine and walked each other home. Jackie and Theo dropped everyone off. They lived in the same neighborhood, so they would walk home together. Theo and his girlfriend kiss goodnight, as Jackie and him walk back in silence.

"So..., thanks," Theo says.

"For what?" Jackie asks, looking forward.

"For lying for me, you didn't have to, and I swear it'll be the last—"

"Theo," she says, facing him, "You didn't tell her that we kissed like three days ago?"

"I didn't, but—"

"Theo, you told me that you two fought, broke up and that we were good. You lied to me, and you keep lying to her."

He's silent. They stand in the middle of the road, only the street lights illuminating their faces. He's looking for some excuse and possibly a way to apologize, but Jackie's full of horror. A look too dark to even describe.

"You made me become the thing I hated most in the world."

She rubs her eyes, trying her best not to cry.

"And the worst part was that I lied for you, and I keep lying for you!" She exclaims

"Jackie, listen. I'm sorry. I'll tell her. I will." He reaches for her, but she pushes him back.

"Tell her for her sake, and never talk to me again. I'm done lying for you and I'm done protecting you."

She walks off towards her house, not looking back. Theo stands there in the road looking as her back disappears.

No matter what lies he tells himself every day it won't matter. He can lie and lie to himself, but he can't lie to others and get away with it all the time.

THE IMAGINARY FRIEND

"We have reasons to believe
that he wasn't there."

48. the imaginary friend

"Darling, how long have you been seeing him?"

"We were playing on the field late at night before school started," she says, swinging her legs on the couch.

"Okay, and did you ever see his face that night?"

"No. It was dark and I was helping him find his flashlight."

"Well, that was very nice of you."

They're in a small room. The wallpapers have dolphins with hideous smiles and big palm trees. She's sitting across from the lady with the pointy glasses and the red nails asking the questions. Her parents stand behind her; both full of concern.

"Am I in trouble?" She asks, looking back at her parents now.

"No honey, not at all. We just want to understand," her mother says, moving as if to comfort her. Her father holds her back.

"What led you to the woods?" The lady continues.

"He did," she says.

"He did what?"

She sighs as if they don't get it. They don't and won't get it.

* * *

It was a few days after school had started. She was out in her backyard after she finished all her schoolwork, then she heard a knock at the back gate. She went over to check.

"Who is it?" She called.

A few seconds later, a red flashlight was thrown over the fence. She was giggling when she pulled open the gate.

* * *

"What was wrong with him?" The pointy-glasses lady scribbles.

"Nothing was wrong with him. He has a disease and he can't go out in the sun." She crosses her arms defensively.

"I understand, but you still couldn't see his face?"

* * *

She noticed that he had a ski mask on. She giggled a little at his paperboy hat with a bow tie to match. He looks like a little gentleman, she thought as he stood there.

"It must be hot under there," she said, as she pointed to his ski mask specifically.

"The doctors say I have to wear it 'cause of my skin condition," he said, looking down at his shoes, "you wanna play?"

"Yea, one sec. Come in," she held the gate open for him.

He ran inside quickly and she called out to her parents that she was gonna play with her friend. Not waiting for an answer as she ran out with him.

* * *

"Oh, it's all my fault, I should've seen him. I should've checked," the mother cries into her husband's shirt.

"Mommy, it's okay. I'm safe now. I'm not hurt. He didn't hurt me."

"Honey, he doesn't exist," her father says, not taking it anymore.

"Yes, he does. You guys scared him off."

* * *

They ran down the grassy hill trying to catch butterflies. Other kids were close by, they joined them for a game of tag, then he asked her if she wanted to see something cool. Hand in hand they walked off towards the woods.

"I saw it a few days ago. I hope it's still here," he said, hopping over fallen trees. He helped her over some rocks.

They made it to a clearing where a rock was leaning against a tree. They climbed up and looked in the hole.

❊ ❊ ❊

"We saw baby owls. I thought they were so cute." She giggles at the memory only she can see.

"How late was it?"

"I don't know. The sun was down, and I forgot to bring my flashlight, but he had his."

❊ ❊ ❊

They were leaning on the rock. She looked over at him.

"Can I see your face?" She asked quietly.

"You can't," he said, looking away and at his shoes again. He shined the light over them, "My Dad told me that if anyone saw my face they'd die."

"I'm sorry," she said.

"It's okay. I don't want you to die. I like you. I think you're cool."

He reached for her hand. This made her smile. She liked him too.

"It's getting late, I'll walk you home." He said letting go.

Her eyelids *were* getting heavy.

"I think I'm gonna nap here," she yawns, tired all of the sudden.

"No, we have to go. Hey, stay awake," he said, trying to shake her, but she soon fell asleep.

* * *

"That's when you guys found me."

"Honey, where'd he go? He wasn't there when we found you." The father says at her side now.

"You guys probably scared him off." She's starting to get angry with them.

"We have reasons to believe that he wasn't there." The lady says like she's stupid.

"Stop lying!" She commands the lady.

"Honey..." The lady tries as her parents jump at their daughter's sudden outburst.

"Stop calling me that. He's real. He's real, and I couldn't see his face, or I would've died, but he didn't want to hurt me. Where is he? I wanna see him!" She screams now.

Her mother starts to cry, the lady starts to walk over to her, and the dolphins wouldn't stop grinning at her. Someone reaches to grab her as they watch.

I HARDLY KNEW HIM

"No, you don't think that he has anything to do with it?"

49. i hardly knew him

The Detective decided to investigate further into the missing librarian. Might as well, because it seems like he's gonna be here for a while. While panic ensues around him, he tries his best to keep himself sane. Lying down on his hotel bed now as he reviews his notes.

"She doesn't have family here, though she has numbers written down that could be friends or relatives out of town. She never takes sick days, no days off, first to arrive last to leave. 35 years of age and was last seen with her boyfriend Ian." He mumbles to himself.

He gets up, opening the patio door to smoke. It's not a whole lot to go off of, and the town's word means crap. All they did was talk about how kind she is, how lovely, how hard-working yadda yadda. He looks out over the town, sighing, and puts out his cigarette to head inside.

"We don't know anything about Ian besides that he was a bodyguard," the girl said to him earlier.

A lead, pretty weak sauce, but a lead. His eyes begin to droop and before he knows it, he's asleep.

✳ ✳ ✳

Morning comes too fast, but it's time for him to head out to town hall.

"Sir, the mayor is pretty busy at this time, you'll need an appointment," a secretary gets up to follow him.

"Didn't know I needed an appointment when the whole world was going to hell." He keeps his pace as she scuttles behind him.

She puffs up as if to say something, but the mayor walks out and down the stairs to meet them.

"It's okay. I have a minute," she looks him up and down, "Alright, follow me please."

He follows close behind her as she leads him to an empty boardroom. She takes the one chair closest to him. A good sign that she wants to listen to him.

"I won't take too long. Now I heard that you had an employee under the name of Ian Dominic?"

"Yes, he was part of the security staff." She nods.

"Was?" He stops his notes to look up.

"Well I dismissed him," she rests her chin on her hands, thinking it over, "I could tell that his heart wasn't in it anymore."

"How so?"

"He just seemed done with my former staff and me. He has a girlfriend, the librarian Ellie, sweet girl. I guess he's found his true calling to her." She shrugs.

"Did you hear that she's missing?"

"Oh no, that's horrible." She gasps.

He watches her grip her heart.

"I had no idea, especially now." She goes on, thinking how could she not notice.

"I understand ma'am, but Ian is also missing."

She pauses. A horrifying look spreads across her face.

"No, you don't think that he has anything to do with it?"

"I don't want to jump to conclusions, but a lot of the town admitted to not knowing anything about him." He leans forward at this last part.

"Listen Detective, I love this town. I really do, but not everyone has to know everything about everyone. It's ridiculous how nosy people can be sometimes. How can we make assumptions based on what we don't know about a person?" She looks at him, eyes like daggers. They hit their intended mark. Noted, he thinks.

"My honest opinion, he didn't kidnap her. Troubled boy, but he loves her." She speaks after a second.

"Love can be blind and dangerous." He counters.

"True, but it can also be our most powerful weapon," she gets up, "I'll give you files on his background if that'll help." She walks off before he could say thank you.

✽ ✽ ✽

Reading in the woods now, it's almost noon, maybe twenty minutes 'til. The woods is where Ian sometimes goes jogging, or where they'd hike most likely. He wasn't looking for anything in particular, but most people who willingly go jogging in the woods have to be hiding something, he thinks.

He passes by an arch and a wood carving of a woman, but no tattered clothes, no shoes, nothing. He looks down for his lighter when he slips on a pile of leaves down a hill.

"Jeez," he says, looking back up the hill, and looking where he landed near an abandoned warehouse.

"Well, this looks promising."

The door creaks open and slams shut as he enters. Clicking on his flashlight he walks around, expecting a torture dungeon. Instead, he finds what looks to be a small replica of the town.

Everything and everyone in this town, down to the mole on the chin of the mayor in her office. This is unsettling, he thinks. He flashes the light over the edge of town and there's a small pickup truck, two figures inside. Pulling up a picture of both Ian and Ellie, there they were just like their figures leaving town, but they seem to be stopped by a spill.

He flashes his light over the town again. Everyone in their spots, just as they described the incident when it happened. He checks a clock in the town square. It reads noon. Checking his own watch, it's ten minutes to noon.

"Crap," he pushes his way out the door and into the woods, climbing the hill for dear life.

"Would you like to hear
a secret?" She whispers.

50. tell no soul

The woman who was under the stairs wasn't expecting to end up in prison. She was surprised to see the little girl, but she couldn't help but smile. It was all coming together, she had thought when they pushed her into the cop cruiser.

Soon enough they'll send in someone to ask her questions. It was all making sense to her now. Soon, she smiles as a pair of footsteps echo down the hall to where she waits.

They buzz him in, but he doesn't see her at first on her side of the glass. He sits down across two inches of glass and a phone on his right. He waits, reaching down to grab his notepad. He looks up to her suddenly sitting across from him. He jolts a little but plays it off as stretching.

She picks up her phone and speaks into it. A warm smile on her face, as he picks up his.

"What was that?" He asked.

"Hello David. They told me you were coming. Sorry I couldn't find anything nice to wear, hope you like orange," she cackles.

He brushes off the fact that she knows his name.

"Ma'am, I'm part of an investigation on

what happened to Ellie the librarian."

"Hmm, I didn't think the town cared about her like that," she says with a shrug.

"Why is that?"

"Well, underappreciated, underpaid, never respected, but the minute she goes "missing" they need her. What a strange little town, huh?" She asks.

"You used air quotes around missing, do you know what happened to her?"

"Oh dear, she isn't missing. She left with him, Ian. They're in love and she needed a change of scenery." She says it like it's a fact they all should know.

"As much as I would like to believe you—"

"I know I haven't built up much of a case for me, but you know why you can believe me, don't you?"

She was talking about her warehouse in the woods, he thinks.

"Ahh, so you do know. Well, what do you think?" She claps her hands, the guard behind her tenses.

"Of your replica?"

"My masterpiece. Took years, but I perfected it, didn't I? Down to every detail. That's why you're here aren't you?" She tilts her head, piles of hair spilling over her shoulder, "You don't care about Ellie or anyone in this town do you?" She asks.

No hate or malice in her voice. Just stating a

fact.

"You caught me, is it wrong that I wanna get out of this town?" He acts along, though he won't deny that she's right.

"Not at all, but I can't help you?"

"Yes, you can. You predicted this day happening, and you're telling you can't alter anything?"

"Young man, the future of thousands is not up to me to alter. Only I can change my own future." She smiles sadly.

"Yea, well none of us are gonna have a nice future." He holds her gaze with an angry one.

"Well, think for a second Davie. Many things happened on that day to alter this rift in time. You should go back and check the board."

He took pictures of every inch of the diorama before meeting her. Nothing out of the ordinary he could spot, there were two people in the woods around noon. Maybe it's the woods. It has to be, but then again this was a hunch.

"Would you like to hear a secret?" She whispers.

"I'm done talking to you." He starts to hang up.

"It'll be worth your while, come on what do you have to lose? It might be a clue."

He hesitates but puts his ear back to the phone. Her face turns down and leans close to the glass, he finds himself leaning forward too.

"You must swear to never tell a soul."

"I swear."

"On your life?" She asks.

He doesn't say anything, but once again as if reading his mind, she smiles.

"To restore the balance of nature, something not from nature has to be destroyed for good. One for the other. You understand?"

"I think so."

"You know Davie, that's a big risk messing with something you don't understand. You get to leave at the end of the day, but the people have to live with the choice you pick. But you know what you have to do." She smiles one last time.

She hangs up the phone, saying one last thing as she walks away with the guard. He watches her walk off . She said "price". What price? Whose to pay? Was it his?

Outside it's late afternoon. He gets a call from his phone. The mayor's number flashes across his screen. Answering it, he walks off in the direction of the woods.

ACKNOWLEDGEMENT

When I first started working on this book, I figured I could get away with writing it and assume everything would fall into place. The one main thing I gained from working through all the steps is that it is a lot more work than that. Besides the editing, illustrating, and more editing I've also learned that it's a lot of fun. It hasn't been easy, but it would've been a whole lot more difficult without my amazing team. I'd like to thank Tishona Watson, my mom, for editing, critiquing, and overall encouragement during this process. Thank you to Avery Phillips for your help in illustrating, I know you'll do great things. A big, big thanks to my father Bobby Phillips. He is the main reason I'm here writing this today and my greatest ally. I love you all more than words can ever covey. This is our book.

ACKNOWLEDGEMENTS

ABOUT THE AUTHOR

Jaelyn Phillips

Jaelyn Phillips is a writer from Ashburn, Virginia. She majors in English for Virginia Commonwealth University. This is her first novel that she's completed with the help of her father, mother, and sister.